To Brooklyn
Go for the Stars
Jeanne Taylor Thomas

KERRY

MCDANIELS

BLOOD RED

MOON

BOOK 3

by

JEANNE TAYLOR THOMAS

"A heartwarming series that will take you
through a spiritual journey."

Darby Briar, award-winning author

Kerry McDaniels Blood Red Moon

All Rights Reserved

Copyright 2014 Jeanne Taylor Thomas

Discover other titles by Jeanne Taylor Thomas at jeannetaylorthomas.com

This is a work of fiction. The event and characters described within are imaginary and are not intended to refer to specific places or living persons. The opinion expressed in this manuscript are solely the opinions of the author and do not represent the opinions or thoughts of the publisher.

This book may not be reproduced, transmitted, or stored in whole or in part by any means, including graphic, electronic, or mechanical without the express written consent of the author except in the case of brief quotations

JEANNE TAYLOR THOMAS

ISBN-9780692298558

PRINTED IN THE UNITED STATES OF AMERICAN

DEDICATION

To my fans who I love, and continually thank

for their support.

ACKNOWLEDGMENTS

Cass Abbott and Richard Palazzolo my beta readers. Andrea Roylance for her suggestions, opening my eyes to seeing things in a different way.

Kerry Thomas and Tami Prickett's constant push to finish this book and help with my book signings.

Karen Devall for the beautiful cover.

OTHER BOOKS BY JEANNE

TAYLOR THOMAS

KERRY MCDANIELS AND THE CAVE   BOOK 1

Kerry and Shadow find the cave. Kerry discovers he shares his soul with an ancient Blackfeet Shaman, Moon Dancer.

KERRY MCDAIELS QUEST   BOOK 2

Kerry leaves for Havre, MT to learn how to use his gifts with the help of his Spirit Animals. Shawgun, the demon skin-walker, sends his puppets to kill Kerry and retrieve what Kerry has to regain his power.

LOVE CAN BE MAGIC

AUSTIN AND HARLOW'S FIRST ADVENTURE

Kerry McDaniels

BLOOD RED MOON

CHAPTER ONE

Book 3

The room was quiet except for Shadow and Brother Wolfs strained breathing and the wind shaking the shutters on the small veterinarian hospital. Only a few hours left before explaining my predicament to my family. What could I tell them to make them understand finishing this journey was no option, no matter what the outcome might be? Separating Moon Dancer's Soul from mine was imperative. Thinking back over the past few months my story sounds like science fiction.

"Kerry let your mind rest, and the words will come when you need them, "sighed Moon Dancer. *"Your body needs to focus on healing, let go and sleep."*

I exhaled. Relax, that was easy for Moon Dancer to say, the ancient Blackfeet Shaman, who shared my mind and half my soul. He did not have to face my parents and my siblings and explain to them how I have kept things from them. Things to keep them safe.

My world had changed since finding that cave, which initiated my dream walking. It is not every day you have to kill a demon and save the girl you love from a blood sacrifice. Relax? Sure!

Lying on the vet table with only a sleeping bag between my skin and the steel tabletop, I sensed the light coming through the window on my closed eyelids. The door opened and shut and then I felt the blankets lift and warm fingers explore around the wound on my leg.

"Harley is that you?" I mind spoke keeping my eyes closed.

"Yes Kerry. You can open your eyes. I am alone for a moment. How are you feeling?"

"Sick."

"Can I get you anything?"

"Nothing, unless you can speed up time and put facing my family behind me."

Harley chuckled. "I'm afraid I can't do that, Kerry," he said removing the old bandage from around my leg where the half-inch stick had claimed entrance and partially exited out the backside. "Your leg is looking good." Throwing the old bandage in the garbage, he put another poultice around my injury. "Before you go into breakfast Josh will be out to look at your wolf bites."

"I'm glad I didn't wake up to the family lying on this table. I need every advantage when talking to them. It would be nice if Jace brought me out clean clothes."

"Someone mention my name?" Jace asked walking into the Veterinarian Hospital followed by cold frosty air.

"Hi," I said looking at the bundle of clothes he carried. "I was hoping when you came out you would bring me clean clothes." I watched him set the bundle down at the end of the table.

"How are you feeling?" He asked and continued over to where Shadow and Brother Wolf lay. He pulled back the curtain so I could see my companions.

"Stronger than last night."

"Shadow, are you awake?" I mind spoke.

"Yes. I'm tired, very tired, but I'm doing better?"

"Brother Wolf?"

"I need to get back to my mate as soon as I can. She waits for me beyond the tree line."

"Mom has fed her so she won't need to hunt. She is safe," I say

"Jace, how do their wounds look? Brother Wolf says he needs to get back to his mate."

"Ask him if he will stay until tonight and if the healing continues he'll be okay to leave. If Josh didn't get all the poison out and since the events have tied their health to yours, making sure there is no relapse in you is imperative," Jace stated.

Relaying the message to Brother Wolf, he agreed to stay until nightfall. Watching Jace, check the IV in Shadow and Brother Wolf was another reminder how close the three of us came to dying. After, he looked over their demon wolf bites they had received in the cave protecting me.

The frigid air sweeps into the room again when Josh comes in.

"How does his leg look, Harley?" Josh asked walking over to the table.

"His leg looks good and I have finished putting on the new poultice. He can sit up and get his pants on before he has any more visitors." Harley said with a big grin.

"I've asked everyone to stay in the house and we would bring Kerry in shortly. Your mom is fixing blueberry pancakes. Your favorite she told me."

"I am awful hungry," I say as my stomach growled.

"Let's take a look at those wolf bites," Josh said helping me remove my shirt.

"A couple more logs wouldn't hurt in that pot-bellied stove either," I suggested as the goose bumps appeared with the removal of my flannel shirt.

"The new tissue around the bites looks good," Josh said to Harley. "How did the hole in his leg look.

"It's closing, and the skin tissue looks healthy," he said. "We're going to help you down Kerry. You will have some dizziness, and you may need a cane for a couple of days. Here we go."

I stepped down on the rug my brother Jace had laid out for me. My leg throbbed for a minute and then I asked for my pants.

"You brought me pajamas. Where are my jeans?"

"We thought these would be best for today. Tomorrow you can wear your jeans if you're feeling up to it," Harley said handing me the sweats and a pair of gym shoes.

Knowing I didn't have much time to heal, I did not argue.

"Kerry, last night when we went to the house, your dad and brothers were discussing the things that have happened. It was an opportunity to tell them about the legend. The legend of my Great, Great, Grandfather Moon Dancer and the one we have been waiting for to fulfill the prophecy," Josh said and continued helping me into my sweats. "I have given them something to think about. When you tell them about your mission, it will be easier for them to accept. Jace, Harley, Nakiya and I will vouch for you."

My cheeks simmered red helped into my pants. I could add that to my list of embarrassing moments.

"No matter the outcome with my family I know I have to face the demon Shawgun and retrieve Moon Dancer's last gift." Grasping the table for balance made it easier to slip my coat on. "I will stay on task and not let my emotions sidetrack me as they have in the past. I'm ready."

"Kerry remember I'm close and so are your other spirit guides," Shadow reassured me.

I looked back at him on the table knowing my foolishness had jeopardized our lives. *"I will be strong,"* I confirmed.

"Moon Dancer, are you awake? I am going to the house now to tell my parents our story. I need you to be alert."

"I'm awake Kerry. Truth is on your side. Besides, you have a brother who believes in you as well as your friends. Think of the outcome you want, and it will happen," he said.

The icy air hit me as I hobbled out of the veterinarian hospital. Jace at my side for support, while Josh and Harley followed us. The smell of bacon cooking and the aroma of coffee greeted us when we reached the backdoor. My chest expanded filling my lungs with fresh air and exhaled slowly before we walked into the house.

Mom stopped what she was doing and rushed over to me. Putting her hands on my cheeks, she looked into my eyes and held my gaze for several moments. It was as if she could look inside me, and I concealed nothing. I had been hiding things far too long from my family.

Mom knew more than what she let on but other than Jace, everyone else was in the dark about Moon Dancer, Shawgun, Dark Antelope and Nakiya. Well, I guess they had surmised my feelings for Nakiya.

Mom put her arms around my neck. "Are you going to be okay? We thought we had lost you," she cried. "I don't want to go through that again."

I felt her tears against my neck and put my arms around her.

"I'm going to be all right, but I have to finish this task given me, or all our lives are in jeopardy." She pushed herself an arm's length away and studied my face. I could see the fear and concern in her eyes. She shook her head up and down acknowledging that I spoke the truth.

"Sit down and have some breakfast," she said leading me to the table. "You need to build your strength." She looked at the others and motioned them to sit down with me. "Dad and your brothers will be in shortly. They're out doing chores."

I looked up when Danene and Nakiya entered the dining area. Danene, my sister, did not hesitate to come over giving me a sisterly hug. Nakiya stood back; I did not encourage her with an invitation to do otherwise. As badly as I wanted to wrap my arms around her, I stood my ground, knowing my feelings for her had landed me in the mess I was recovering from lack of discipline. I sat down. My stomach growled. That was a good sign I was on the mend.

Danene brought me a cup of coffee and set it down when the back door opened. The chilled draft entered with Dad, Rob and Steve. Rob was my oldest sibling followed by Steve, Danene and Jace. I am the youngest.

"We have a heck of a storm coming in from the North West," Dad commented taking off his coat and overshoes. "I wouldn't be surprised by the first of January we have snow sticking to the rock face of the Cabinets."

I almost choked on my coffee. The Cabinets are a high rocky mountain range about fifteen miles away and somewhere up there; Shawgun waited. That was too soon. If the storm were only two weeks away, how could I be completely healed in time? I had not even translated the writings Mr. Chavez had given me. The secret that would enable me to vanquish the skin-walker. My gear was still in town at Mr. Granger's café. As Dad approached, I was apprehensive.

"Gosh, it's good to have you home," he said pulling me up from my chair. I cringed as his hands gripped me, adding pressure to my wounds. Held in his embrace, I tried to forget the pain.

"I'm sorry Dad."

"You're alive and home and that's all I care about."

"Well, it's not all I care about," Steve shouted. "Kerry what the heck is going on? And what was that ungodly scream we heard twice last night?" He asked spilling the cup of coffee Danene set on the counter. "Sorry Sis," and turned his attention back to me.

Watching Danene wipe up the hot liquid, averted my attention from my brother. She quickly had the coffee cleaned up, was refilling Steve's cup. How simple her effort, two swipes of her hand and the liquid disappeared. She then poured Rob one as well. Why couldn't things be that easy?

With his cup in hand, Rob stepped up beside Steve, both watching me intently.

"Those wolves that attacked you and we killed had red eyes. I have never seen a wolf with red eyes. I'm sure you know something about them, too," Rob pitched in.

"That's enough," Mom said sternly. I will not have this hostility in my house. After breakfast, Kerry will answer your question. Go wash your hands and come sit down."

Everyone turned toward Mom, shocked at hearing her raise her voice. I heard the water go on in the mudroom, and those in the dining room pulled our chairs out. Danene and Nakiya help her put the food on the table and fill the remaining coffee cups. Water stopped, and the mudroom door shut. With everyone seated, I was surprised that Mom spoke first as Dad usually said grace.

"Dear Lord, we thank thee for thou bounty that we receive. We thank thee for the food that is before us that it will nourish our minds and bodies. We thank thee for the love in this family and the friendship we share with those around us. We ask that our hearts and minds will be open to the things we hear this day and that thou will guide us in our action. In the name of our Lord Jesus Christ. Amen."

We ate breakfast in silence, unusual for our family. Mom's food always tasted great but right now, it felt like lead in my belly. My leg was throbbing. I was worried since Harley had put a clean dressing on before we come into the house. When he attended my wounds at the taxidermy school from the grizzly attack, the pain had been minimal. I guess that was because Josh had left him herbs to give me to make me sleep. That did not happen this time. Now I felt every pump of my heart go through my leg, and the tension in the room grew along with my anxiety.

"We can leave the dishes for later. Let's all go into the family room," Mom said standing by my side. "Take your coffee with you if you'd like. Kerry would you like some water or coffee refill?"

"Water will be fine, Mom." My throat already felt dry before I started talking.

"I'll be right back. Stay here," she said.

When she comes back, I stood up as she took hold of my arm. She smiled briefly. We followed Harley and Josh into the family room and sat down. Before anyone could start asking question, Mom stated.

"I believe the best route is to let Kerry start from the beginning and we hold our question until he is through with his story. Agreed?"

Reluctantly heads bobbed up and down in agreement. Steve rolled his eyes. The rest were not happy. They knew better than to go against Mom's request.

"We'll listen, but I want you to know you're not leaving this ranch until spring," Dad stated.

"Now Jacob, let's hear what he has to say before we make any rash declarations," she said putting her arm around my father's shoulder as she sat on the arm of the large leather chair my dad occupied.

'To start my story I need to go back to when I was six. That may sound strange, but that's when my story begins that brings me to this time."

My siblings looked at each other as Danene shrugged her shoulders.

"Remember on my sixth birthday you gave me a camera. I took that camera outback to capture the squirrel that had been my automatic alarm clock for the last year. When he started down the tree, I put the camera up to my eye and asked him if I could take his picture. Jokingly of course, I never expected to get an answer." I paused and took a sip of water.

"The squirrel said sure how do you want me to pose. I was so shocked when I heard a voice in my head that I fell backward over a stump. The squirrel laughed. Getting back up I looked at him curiously. Looking around to see if any of you were close, I gathered my courage and asked him if he had talked to me? He told me of course he had. Again, he asked me how I wanted him to pose. I told him and took the picture."

I saw Nakiya get up and go down the hallway. A minute later, she returned with a picture from off my dresser. She gave it to me and sat back down. I turned the picture around so everyone could see.

"You're joking right?" Steve laughed, shaking his head. "That's a fairy tale if I ever heard one."

Steve was the logical one. If there was not scientific proof behind something, it did not exist. I could tell Rob wanted to say something, but after looking over at Mom, he took another swallow of his coffee.

"Go on Kerry," Mom urged.

"If you remember after that first week, I put my camera away and didn't use it again until I was twelve. Danene was having trouble getting good shots of the animal life to take to the Outfitter Shows her and Dad were doing. Therefore, I thought I would try it. If what happened before, happened again, I sure as heck was not going to tell anyone this time. Well, it happened again, and I did not say anything to any of you. You have some beautiful shots that everyone thought took me hours to take. Besides, the photos brought a lot of business to the ranch. I kept my secret that I could talk to the animals with my mind, and I only did it when I used my camera."

"It's true," said Jace. "I've seen him do it. He talks to Shadow all the time."

"Yes, I talk to Shadow, but it wasn't until we found the hidden cave that I was able to talk to him and my first spirit animal, White Wolf."

"The cave you said you seen the pictographs on the walls. The one with the wolf carved in the ceiling looking down at us?" Rob asked. "Are you the only one who can see those, too?"

"No," stated Jace. "I saw all of them when I stayed the night inside that cave with Kerry."

"Nakiya and I have seen all of them, also," commented Josh. Nakiya shook her head in agreement.

"Does this have anything to do with the legend you told us about last night, Josh?"

Dad asked rubbing his hand on the chair fabric.

"Yes sir, I'm afraid it does."

Dad sank deeper into his chair and leaned to the side until his forehead was resting in the palm of his hand.

"This is ridiculousness," Steve blinked and scooted to the front of his seat.

Dad raised his hand. "Hold on a minute Steve. I know you believe nothing exist between your left and your right. Kerry is your brother, and I have never known him to lie. Let's finish listening to what he has to say."

Steve started to open his mouth again before Dad sat up straight in his chair. Steve sat back into the sofa and motioned me to continue with the wave of his hand.

"The cattle killings were because of me."

"What! Steve yelled and jumped up from his seat.

"Jace I think we are going to need one of those sedatives Doc left for Kerry. Your brother's blood pressure is not going to take much more. I have a feeling this story is going to get worse before it gets better."

"Don't you even think about it, Jace? I don't take pills," Steve threatened. "I think I'll get me something out of Dad's desk that he keeps for special guest. If you'll excuse me for a minute and don't say another word until I get back."

Steve returned with a glass of golden brown liquid but instead of sitting, he stood against the doorjamb to the hallway.

"Kerry, why didn't you say something?" Rob said harshly. I'd say that was a vital piece of information to keep secret?"

"I was afraid of putting you all in harm's way. I didn't know if Shawgun would only kill the cattle or go after one of you, Rob."

"Shawgun?" Rob asked his eyebrows pinched together.

"I'll get to him," I say. I could feel the perspiration prickle on my forehead.

"Anyone need their cup refreshed? Mom asked looking around the room. "Girls would you help me? I think we'll have to brew another pot."

"Kerry, Mr. Granger sent your things back with me when I took Doc home. He gave me a large box and said it wasn't to be opened by anyone but you," Dad said. I believe he was trying to defuse the tension building.

I thought Dad would get more upset than Steve would. Surprising what you find out about family in a crisis.

"Jace would you get my knife and the arrowhead out of my bag before everyone is back? Oh, and would you bring in that box Dad was talking about." I was feeling lightheaded. My blood pounded in my wounds as a steady drum beat. "Mom can I have a glass of orange juice?" I was exhausted. How much more of my story would be told resembled the last sands in an hourglass.

"It was in the cave I learned half my soul belongs to Moon Dancer an ancient Blackfoot Shaman. In fact, Moon Dancer is Josh and Nakiya's Great-Great- Grandfather. He talks to me and shares space in my head." Steve and Rob's jaw fell, their eyes sprung wide open, and their expressions would have been comical, if the situation were not serious.

"Moon Dancer's sister, Spotted Fawn, was kidnapped by a small renegade band from the South West. They were going to use her for a blood sacrifice, however, Moon Dancer was able to follow them and rescue her. In the box canyon, Moon Dancer set it on fire after he retrieved Spotted Fawn. Shawgun died in the fire along with four braves that were with him. He shouted his last words at Moon Dancer. He cursed him and promised that he would sever his ties with his people forever."

I had taken a drink of orange juice before I continued letting the cold citrus run slow over my parched throat.

"When Moon Dancer and his sister Spotted Fawn made it back to their country they found a cave and stayed there while Moon Dancer recovered from his injuries. He buried a knife in that cave, and I found it when I was digging a hole for my stash. Jace was there when I found it. It was the same knife given to me in my dream." I took the knife holding it fondly then gave it back to Jace so he could pass it around for everyone to see.

"Before it was time for Moon Dancer to cross over he hid his special gifts the Great One had given him so he could reclaim them again when he was reborn. A demon Shawgun had been watching, and when Moon Dancer crossed over, Shawgun stole Moon Dancer's gifts. Gifts Shawgun has hid from Moon Dancer's people."

"That is part of the story Josh told us last night," Danene spoke wrapping her arms around her. She looked over at Josh and then me, her face paled. "Something happened at the powwow didn't it? You were never the same Kerry when you came home."

"Yes. I met Wolf Talker, their shaman great grandfather. I went through one of their scared ceremonies." I opened my shirt and showed them the scars from the Sun Dance ceremony.

Mom gasped but stayed silent. I knew she would want every detail when we were alone.

"It was Josh that figured out that each time I had a dream in the cave that it correlated with the cattle killings. Shawgun felt our vibration and would have a temper tantrum. He fears us." I said my words almost a slur.

"Kerry I think you need to rest. Your color is getting ashen," Josh stated. "The poison we extracted was powerful and it is going to take a few days before you regain your strength."

"I'll continue later. I'm just so tired."

Josh and Jace were at my side when I tried to stand, but failed. They lifted me up and carried to the davenport Mom had made up for me. I felt my shoes removed the covers pulled over my shoulders. Drifting in and out of sleep half listening to the conversation going on in the house, brought me to the concussion that a deep sleep would escape me.

CHAPTER 2

Mom spoke softly. "Is he going to be alright, Josh?" I heard her ask and continued to listen keeping my eyes closed.

"Yes Mrs. McDaniels. He just needs to sleep. As I told him, it would take a while to rebuild his strength. The poison used was powerful, and he should have died. Kerry is strong besides his spirit animals watch over him."

"Josh, please call me Sally. I think we are past being formal. You feel like part of the family now."

Yes, he did, I agreed silently.

"I wasn't sure how you would feel about Nakiya and me after hearing part of Kerry's story," Josh said standing with his thumbs hooked in his back pockets.

"You didn't plan this. So why would you think I'd blame you Josh?"

"I guess I've been around to many whites that like to blame my people for things they don't understand."

Jace asked picking up a cookie on his way to the mudroom. "I'm going to check on our other patients. Would you like to come along Harley?"

"Coming," Harley, replied.

"Harley, I have another roast for Brother Wolf's mate. You can take it out to her; I doubt she will wonder too far away from him. I put it on top of the freezer in the pantry last night."

Smiling graciously, he replied, "Thank you Mrs. McDaniels. She will enjoy another meal without having to hunt. Her mate will appreciate her being taken care also."

"As I've told Josh, my name is Sally and we aren't formal around here. Especially with people we hold dear," she said stretching the taut muscles in her neck. "I've always known Kerry had special talents. I didn't know how to help him develop them," she said barely above a whisper. "I'm going to go lie down, too."

Josh and Harley looked at each other, silent exchange between them. Harley went to the pantry first before joining Josh putting on his winter gear. Jace was already out the door.

"I knew that Sally was gifted, but to what extent I don't know. She has in the past. Kerry told me she knew things would happen before they actually transpired." stated Josh. "Perhaps when this is over I will sit down with her." They put on their heavy coats and their boots after which Harley picked up the thawed elk roast he had set on the bench.

"I thought I saw Brother Wolf's mate early this morning by those two large pines over there. I'll just be a minute." Harley searched again for the female wolf. When he spied her, she stood up cautiously, not taking her eyes off him. *"Your mate will be back with you tonight."*

Her head jerked up as she flinched when he mind spoke to her.   He halted ten feet away, tore the wrapper off the meat and tossed it near her feet, then backed up slowly. She stayed where she was coming forward to sniff the meat only after he was back near the vet hospital.

Going inside Harley shuffled over to the woodbin picked up three logs and put them in the potbelly stove. Taking off his gloves, he rubbed his hands together feeling the warmth spew into the room from the old stove. Gradually he made his way over to where Jace stood.

"Shadow, how are you feeling?" Harley asked looking over Jace's shoulder at the shaved areas of the pinkish wounds.

"Tired so tired, like I've run a 100 miles," he whispered.

"*I think as Kerry's strength increases yours and Brother Wolf's will do the same,"* Harley said running his fingers through Shadow's thick coat. "Don't you think so Jace that as Kerry's health strengthens, so will theirs?"

"I hope so," Jace said removing the IV from Shadow.

"Harley," Josh called. "Ask Brother Wolf if I let him go tonight, if he'll stay close to the ranch. If Kerry's health takes a turn for the worse, at least, he'll be close, and

I can help him," Josh continued looking at Brother Wolf's wounds. "The wounds are healing but I don't know how Shawgun has tied their health to Kerry's. I would have thought when we retrieved all the poison out it would have severed any links, and maybe it has." Josh removed the IV from Brother Wolf setting the small tubes in the stainless steel sink.

Harley relayed the message to Brother Wolf and Brother Wolf agreed. Harley knew his main concern was for his mate.

"Sleep both of you. That will help you heal and Brother Wolf. Your mate is cared for, sleep without worry. We can go back. I know Kerry will be hammered with questions," Harley commented.

Josh and Jace agreed.

"Harley, are you going to tell them that you can mind speak with the animals?" Josh asked turning the handle to the door. Snowflakes were falling in swirls as the wind blew from several directions.

"No. They have enough to digest with what Kerry has told them. White minds I believe are more vulnerable than ours are. If it is not tangible, it cannot be real. Most of Kerry's family will accept what he has told them, the others will in time."

"I agree with you," Jace said following them out the door and closing it behind him.

"I need to wake Kerry for lunch," Sally stated.

"I would let him sleep," Nakiya said. "What he ate this morning will be sufficient until dinner."

"Nakiya, were you there when Kerry went through the ceremony?"

"Yes. I was there, and so was Josh."

"Was he in a lot of pain? I've seen wounds and wounds that leave that kind of scarring had to be deep," Sally said as she took the plates down from the cupboard. Tears welled in her eyes.

"He was very brave. To complete the ceremony is a great honor taking a boy into manhood. However, to be first is even a greater honor. My grandfather gave him his Blackfeet name," Nakiya said with pride.

"His Blackfeet name? He has never mentioned that. What is it? Sally asked in awe. "He has kept so much to himself. I should have asked more questions.

"His Blackfeet name is Spirit Walker. It wouldn't have made a difference, Sally," Nakiya replied getting the silverware out of the drawer. "He thought you were all in danger and the less you knew, the safer he kept you."

"Spirit Walker. It has a special meaning?" Sally set the plates on the counter waiting for an answer.

"You will have to ask Kerry, Sally. I think it best he tells you."

"Okay, I will do that." Sally bit lightly on her bottom lip and then asked. "So do you believe in these spirit animals?" she asked walking over to the fridge."

"I do believe in them. I have listened to my spirit animals since I first learned of them as a small child with my grandfather. They will guide him, but it is he and Moon Dancer who have to complete the mission he spoke of."

"Rob I didn't see you standing there," Sally spoke rubbing her hands on her apron."

Rob crossed his arms over his chest and leaned against the fridge. "Nakiya I know your people believe in things beyond this realm. "I'm just having a hard time with something like this happening to someone in my family."

Nakiya strolled over to him placing her hand on his shoulder. "Rob, you have an open mind and that alone will help Kerry. I know he will not tell you everything. His first and foremost thoughts have been to keep you all safe. Your support will help him more than anything else," Nakiya replied.

Rob shook his head up and down without saying anything and went back into the family room.

"I have cold cuts in the fridge and a potato salad. In the pantry, there are chips if you would get those Nakiya." They put the food on the table and called everyone in, everyone except Kerry. It was if a shadow had fallen over the ranch as they were all in their thoughts and lunch went quickly. The merriment of Christmas only a few days away was forgotten, with the absence of a tree.

"I think we should get chores done early tonight so when Kerry awakens we don't have to worry about them," Jacob suggested going to the mudroom to put on his winter coat. We have Daisy to milk, the horses in the barn and east corral and the two steers in the west corral."

"I need to check on Shadow and Brother Wolf again," Josh commented.

"I can milk the cow," offered Harley. "Just tell me where everything is."

"I'll show you Harley. Most everything is in the milk barn. The clean bucket is in the pantry behind the door," Jace replied.

"Got it," Harley said pulling on his gloves the bucket swinging on his arm.

"We'll go out the mud room door. That will keep the cold air from coming into the kitchen," Steve said and led the way. "I'll take care of the steers."

"Check the waterline, Steve," his dad stated. "We wrapped them but it's supposed to get pretty cold tonight.

In fact, we had better check them all. I don't want to have to deal with broken lines over the holidays."

Steve crunched his way through the snow toward the west corral, slowed, as the hair on the back of his neck stood up. *Crap, I should have brought my rifle.* His fingers twitched to hold the gun left in the mudroom. In his peripheral vision, he could see Brother Wolf's mate loping just inside the tree line in his direction. Her growls gave him reason to stop. Searching the tree line for movement before he continued he saw nothing. Hearing the stressed moos of the cows quickened his step forward in their direction. When he reached the corral, the steers were going crazy trying to break down the fence or go over it. Grabbing the lariat on the fence post, he slipped in between fence logs trying to settle the cows to no avail. The howl of the wolf turned his eyes back up to the tree line. Branches snapped as the large grizzly broke through the pines.

"Rob, grab your gun. Hurry," he shouted. The cows fear crazed eyes gave no heed to Steve and rushed pass him knocking him to the ground going over the fence taking two poles down. The ground riveted with the weight of the grizzly as each paw crushed through the snow covered ground. Brother Wolf's mate caught the grizzly's attention as she ran toward him, and he slowed down slightly. Steve hearing the heavy breathing of the bear untangled himself from the lariat and stood up turning to run.

"Hit the ground," Rob yelled as Steve was in his line of fire. Four rounds he put into the grizzly before the fifth took him down crashing over the fence coming nose to nose with Steve.

"Are you alright," Rob yelled running up to where his brother lay in the snow. He pulled him away and as Steve's boots caught traction putting further distance between him and the downed bear.

"Yeah. I think so. Thanks bro," he said brushing off the snow.

Jacob and the others come running around the corner each with a rifle in hand. "You both alright?" Jacob asked continuing over to where the downed grizzly lay. "This is most unusual. The bears should have gone into hibernation with the first snow.

Josh and Harley walked around the large animal. They looked for red eyes, but the eyes were brown.

"I can't guarantee the meat of this grizzly isn't tainted nor the hide is harmless. Until Kerry finishes his mission either burn it or put it in the freezer where no other animals can get to it. Animals eating the meat could fall under Shawguns trance. It's your choice." Josh concluded. Harley shook his head in agreement.

"As much as I hate to waste, I'd rather be safe. Let's burn it," Jacob said. "Let's pull him off the fence. We can re-nail most of it."

It took four of them to drag the grizzly clear so they could burn the carcass. Josh asked them to all step back. He spoke words over the grizzly in his native tongue and then lit it on fire. Moments later a deathly demonic scream of pain roared down from the north pass. Less than three minutes the carcass disappeared. All the men were variable shaken and then looking back at the scorched ground where the carcass had laid. Steve fell to his knees and grasped one of the standing fence posts, his tan skin nearly white as the snow.

"Are you okay son?" Jacob asked his hand on his son's arm.

Steve wiped his brow and spit the blood out of his mouth from his cut lip. "If it hadn't been for that female wolf I wouldn't have had time to yell for help. And to think I tried to kill her," Steve said shaking.

"You need to go into the house?" Rob asked.

"No. We need to get this fence fixed, and the animals tended. I'll be all right. Go get a hammer and some nails," he said pulling himself back up with father's help.

"I'm going to go check the other animals," Jace stated. Harley and Josh were already on their way back to the barns.

"Dad, I think we should put the rest of the horses in the inside riding arena," Rob stated. "Steve may not like it, but if something else comes through those woods, I'd rather they get the two steers we were planning on butchering, than one of those horses I've got sold."

"You're probably right and Steve would agree. Let's go do it."

"Mom what's going on?" Kerry cried out. He sat up and pushed himself against the back of the davenport. "Mom!"

"It's alright Kerry," she soothed. "Whatever it is has been taken care of, I'm sure."

Danene and Nakiya stood in the doorway.

"Danene, fetch me a cold washcloth, please," Mom said pushing my sweaty hair back from my face

"It was Shawgun, Mom. I know it was. I have put you all in danger. I tried not to fall asleep."

"Here Mom," Danene said softly handing the cool washcloth to her mother.

"It's alright Kerry. Your home and we McDaniels stick together." She placed the cold cloth on my forehead.

"Where is everyone? Are they okay? I heard gunshots," I say feeling nauseated.

"They're outside doing chores, and I'm sure as soon as they're finished they'll be in and explain what happened," she soothed.

"I didn't dream. I try hard not to dream, Mom." *My dreams had brought so much destruction to my family's livestock and the ranches around the area. Shawgun retaliating whenever I dreamed walked. I had felt him close.*

"I'm sure you didn't. You've been peacefully sleeping I thought."

Outside the window on the flower box perched an owl.

"Look Kerry, at the window," Nakiya said surprised.

Looking up, I saw Night Eagle looking at me through the glass.

"Be calm, Spirit Walker. Shawgun grows weaker the longer he stays in this realm. He is losing the strength to cast spells. Still powerful, however, I believe he will wait now until you start to hunt him. Rest."

"Thank you Night Eagle. I was afraid he would attack a member of my family."

"Yes, he tried and failed."

"Are you talking to that owl?" Mom asked wonderment show in her blue eyes. "You are, aren't you?"

"Yes Mother. That is Night Eagle, one of my spirit animals." I was surprised he had shown himself.

"Maybe, he's telling us to have a little more faith," Mom said looking at the owl and then me.

CHAPTER 3

All were gathered in the family room once again with the exception of Josh. The fireplace blazed making the room warm and inviting. Mom had made her famous eggnog. The scent of cinnamon fluttered through the air.

"I'm ready to listen to all you have to say," Steve said looking around the room at each of us. "After what happened this afternoon I'm lucky to be here. It might take some time to fathom all that you're going to tell us, but go ahead."

"First, I do have a question," Rob intervened. "We all have heard that horrible death scream or shriek whatever you want to call it, three times. What is it?"

I took a deep breath and let it out slowly. The first time they heard Shawgun they had rescued me from the wolf attack in the cave. Burning the dead wolf carcasses had taken power from Shawgun "That is…" Stopping mid-sentence when the kitchen door opened and shut, I was surprised when Josh and Shadow strolled into the kitchen.

"Shadow, how are you doing?" My heart pumped a bit faster watching him slowly stroll his way to my side.

"Better. Since Brother Wolf went to be with his mate, I thought I would like to sleep in my bed. I agree with you that the table gets harder the longer you lie on it." He

lay down at my feet. *"Continue with your story and if you leave something important out I'll remind you."*

I put my hand on Shadow's back and felt his calming energy flow into me.

"As I was saying that was Shawgun. When he was alive, he was an evil skin-walker from the southwest, who was going to use Moon Dancer's sister Spotted Fawn for a blood sacrifice. When he died in the fire, he became a vile demon skin-walker and traveled between here and Icebis."

"Icebis. What's Icebis?" Dad asked his brow furrowed.

I settled back in my chair. There was no way I was going to explain how I had traveled to Icebis and fought demons to recover Moon Dancer's first gift. "I'll tell you about Icebis another time. Remember when that ranch-hand shot the claw off that grizzly we were hunting, and you wanted to know why Jace and I went to retrieve it?" I ask pulling the claw out from underneath my shirt on its leather strand.

"This claw is the finger of Shawgun in his demon/human form. It protects me from him and keeps him in this realm. At the powwow Wolf Talker, Josh and Nakiya's great grandfather told me never to take it off." I put it back inside my shirt and picked up my cup of eggnog giving everyone time to wrap their heads around my words.

"So you're saying that thing or demon whatever you want to call it, can't kill you to get that part of his body back?" Rob asked staring at me intently.

Leaning forward, I put my forearms on my thighs and glanced around at everyone in the room. "If Shawgun were to kill me to get the claw back he would lose his power. He can send others try to kill me. Like Roger when he pushed me into that snake pit. The grizzly that left me this scar when I was at school in Havre." I held up my shirt showing them the claw rake down my side. I knew they would see the scar eventually "And that phony Sheriff in Havre at the hospital who was looking for the claw. Shadow sensed evil in him and warned me."

Mom laid her hand on her chest and tapped her fingers.

"Besides, not seeing the leather thong around my neck, and Mom's return to my room, the so-called sheriff left. They had removed the claw when they did x-rays."

"I'm a good judge of character, and he didn't sit right with me," Mom explained. "Besides, Jace was so adamant about getting that claw back around your neck it could have been the president in the room with you and I would have gotten it back where it needed to be," Mom said coming over to look at the long pink scar.

"That had to be deep," she said running her fingers over the purple/pink area.

"If it hadn't been for Josh and Harley's medicine skills after that grizzly attack, I'd probably be dead, Mom."

I was starting to feel a little more at ease. Letting them ask questions was easier than going through the whole story I realized. I would be able to keep the things they did not need to know about or would believe, under wraps.

"The wolf attack that was this Shawgun's also doing?" Rob asked shaking his head his face grim.

"Yes, and I believe the first time you heard him scream," I replied.

"Jace none of this seems to be a surprise to you. Have you known all along about Kerry's situation?" Rob asked.

Jace slowly nodded and glanced around the room.

Standing up Rob walked over and stood just a few feet in front of Jace. Jace stood up.

Before anyone could react, Rob hit Jace in the jaw. Cries of alarm sounded around the room. Dazed, Jace fell back into the chair he had been sitting. Steve and Dad jumped up taking hold of Rob's arms.

"Son, stop! This will solve nothing," Dad scowled.

I stood up shocked at Rob. He had always been the levelheaded one. I would have understood it coming from Steve; he had a short fuse sometimes.

Rob pulled away from their hold. "He's put this entire family in danger, besides the hunters who frequent us with their business. Look at the money we have lost with the cattle. We were lucky we did not lose any of the horses. What were you thinking not telling us of the danger we were in?"

"That's my fault. I made Jace promise not to say anything. If you want to hit someone, hit me. I thought it safer if I kept you in the dark about Shawgun. And with me going off to school in Havre, I hoped he would follow me, and you wouldn't be in any danger."

"I believe what Rob is getting at is we haven't kept secrets from each other in the past. We have stood together to overcome any adversity that has come knocking on our door as a family. It wasn't right to withhold that from us." Steve commented stepping away from Rob.

My clenched fists rubbed the sides of my thighs.

"And you would have believed me?" I yelled staggering back. I put my hand on the armchair and sat back down. "You didn't believe me in the cave when the pictographs weren't visible. What makes you think you would have believed my dreams?"

"Spirit Walker calm down," Moon Dancer coaxed. *"They fear for you, that's what brings out this hostility. Speak softly. You don't want Shawgun to think this house is divided feeling the negative energy."*

"You're right Moon Dancer; I'll try harder so they can understand."

"I'm sorry. Let me put the problem to you this way plain and simple," I started with a deep breath. Josh, Harley and Nakiya sat quietly observing. "Shawgun needs his claw to be able to leave earth."

"Leave earth?" Steve questioned his brow crinkled.

I drew my hand through my hair and itched the back of my neck. "Yes. If he does leave with this claw, my soul and Moon Dancer's soul will never separate, and Shawgun will take Moon Dancer's last gift, and hide it forever. He also wants Nakiya for a blood sacrifice to replace the one Moon Dancer prevented."

Nakiya gasped. "No," she exclaimed.

"Shhh… we'll talk of this later Nakiya," Josh stated.

"I'm sorry you're all thrown into this. I didn't ask for it, but I need to see it through to the end." I sat back drained of my energy. The tension in the room was high. My family looked at Nakiya, each other, and then me. You could have heard the wings of a humming bird it was so quiet.

Rubbing his knuckles, Rob stepped further back from Steve. "What is Moon Dancer's last gift that's so important to save?"

"Moon Dancer says when the time is right he will tell me. However, I know better than to put it in my mouth like the gift used in taxidermy. That caused all kinds of …" feeling my throat closing caused a coughing spell.

"Now, is not the time to have them asking about your shape-shifting. You're not strong enough to shift to prove the truth of it," stated Moon Dancer.

"Did you have to choke me?"

"Sometimes I have to use different methods to get your attention."

Danene handed me a glass of water. "You okay."

"Yah. My throats just dry."

"Sally would you make more coffee?" Dad asked walking out of the room. "I'm going to bring in some logs for the fire. Let's take a break."

"Would you all like a piece of apple pie?" Mom asked. "While you mull over what Kerry has told us?"

Harley grinned and followed Mom into the kitchen. "That sounds great," Harley spoke up. "I've heard Kerry talk about your apple pie."

Danene scowled. "Even in desperate times, boys think of their stomachs."

"Kerry, come in the kitchen," she spoke holding the swivel chair at the bar for me to sit on. "You do have a plan to complete this task?"

I looked down at the floor and then back up to my mother's face.

"I don't," I said looking back to Josh and Harley.

Mom followed my gaze. "Do they have a plan? Are they going to be able to help you?"

"They will probably go with me," I said looking down at my hands, "but Moon Dancer and I will have to face Shawgun to eliminate him and find where he hid Moon Dancer's third gift."

Sally sighed looking down at the plates in her hands. "Do you think your brothers are going to sit here and let you go off by yourself again? I don't think so."

I watched Shadow pad slowly to my bedroom.

"Shadow?"

"I'm going to lie down in my bed. All the negative energy is giving me a headache."

"I understand. I'm very tired myself."

"Sally," Harley addressed my mother. "Can I help you with something?"

"Yes, Harley. The pies are in the fridge if you would get them out please."

"Mom I'm really tired. I'm going to go lie down for a bit," I said getting up from the stool taking hold of the cane that Jace had given me to use.

"You don't want a piece of the pie?" she asked taking out the forks from the drawer.

"Maybe later." I shuffled slowly down the hall to my room and after entering, I shut the door. I passed on Mom's apple pie, unbelievable. I did not have the energy to pick up a fork, and I doubt my taste buds would work either.

It was 8 p.m. when I ambled back into the family room. I saw my large box sitting in the middle of the room.

Curiosity, written on everyone's face had Harley smiling knowing what was in the box. Waiting to view the expressions of the others when the box opened, Harley's eyes sparkled.

"Can we see what's in the box that Mr. Granger sent out with your things?" Rob asked. I had noticed him eyeing it several times earlier, more so than the others do.

I grinned as I carefully knelt down beside it. "I would be happy to show you what's inside the box." I decided to wait until they saw my Red Tail Hawk, before telling them I now possessed one of Moon Dancer's gifts. Pulling back the tape, I let the sides of the box fall to the floor. Hearing the gasps, I stood up holding the bird.

"Wow. Why would you keep a live hawk boxed up? It hadn't made a sound the entire time," Steve commented.

"That's because he isn't alive to speak. He was my final project at school."

"I can't believe it. He is beautiful beyond words. He looks like he could lift up and fly," Dad said getting up, he come over and stood by me and lightly touched the hawk's feathers on its chest.

"Let me put him on the dining room table and you can all get a closer look." Walking proudly to the dining room I set him down and backed away giving them space.

Dad rubbed his fingers across his chin going over every detail. "Kerry I knew you would do a great job but this is beyond words," Dad commented.

The black tip of the bird's beak was slightly hooked. The fine yellow down feathers blended into the brown rustic colored feathers, which continued down its back leading into the red tail feathers banded with brown and cream. The light amber eyes were intelligent. The bird's chest covered in shades of light cream and gold with a brown-staggered design and the wings flared back exposing the almost black wing tips were beautiful.

"Is this one of Moon Dancer's gifts you were given?" Mom asked putting her arm around my waist.

"Yes it is. When I was finishing my Red Tail Hawk, I felt a sensation flow through my body as I put my hand on this bird."

"He was able to do the same with mine," Harley spoke up. "That was when Mr. Chavez took Kerry aside and ah...ah...I'll let Kerry tell you about that."

"I was having a rough time in class with Shawgun on my mind and working with my spirit animals on shaa..." *they were not ready to hear about my shape-shifting, so I hurried on.* However, in the end it came together. I thought that just because I had the gift everything would flow with little effort. However, it was not the case. I had to work hard from the first stage to the last stage, and I thought I would never get it down."

"Oh, so the gift was the look of life," Steve said looking closer into the hawks eyes.

"Yes. It's like a part of its soul is given back." *Is that how you would explain it Moon Dancer?*

"Yes that's a good description. If Shawgun had succeeded in hiding that gift, you would have seen less and less realistic taxidermy even among the best practitioners. As you have seen what has been done over the last century, dull and lifeless."

"Kerry?" My father called.

"Sorry, I was listening to Moon Dancer."

"You talk to him in your head?" Rob asked pouring himself a cup of coffee.

"We talk in thought patterns. It was strange getting used to having him inside. He sleeps a lot conserving his energy for when we have to face Shawgun."

"Harley mentioned a Mr. Chavez. Who is he?" Mother asked not wanting anyone to think about Shawgun.

"Mr. Chavez was a teacher at the school. Quiet, but a great instructor. His sister was sacrificed by a skin-walker when he was a small boy. When he was older, a priest gave him a book he said held a prophecy. The priest told him someday he would meet a person who would avenge his sister death. He was to give the book to that person."

"And he gave you this book?" Steve asked sitting back down.

"Yes he did."

"And how did he know to give you this book, Kerry?" Rob asked.

"A person who could give the essence of life into taxidermy work would be the one," I said as the room started to spin.

"Well, you sure have done that. You look pale," Steve commented.

"I'm sorry, but I'm going to have to call it a night," I said. My leg throbbed." I feel light headed, and my strength is faltering. Grasping the corner of the gun cabinet to steady myself

"The poison from the wolf bites would have killed anyone else. If it were not for Kerry's snake spirit, Kerry would not be here. That is why you thought he was dead when you saw him lying on the table in the vet hospital. His snake spirit had to take over his body and with Josh and Nakiya's help they were able to extract the poison," Jace explained.

"Taxing his body, will take him a few days longer to recover all his strength," Josh commented.

"My father told me the happier the energy around Kerry the harder it is for Shawgun to work his dark spells," Harley said.

"Well then, I believe we have put off cutting down our Christmas tree long enough. It's three days until Christmas," Dad said trying to ease the tension in the room "With chores done in the morning, we'll hook the sleigh up and go cut our tree. I have one already marked, and it's only half mile away."

"Nakiya and I can get the decorations out, or do you want to go with them to cut the tree down, Nakiya?" Danene asked.

"I'll stay here. I'd also like to help Sally make a batch of cinnamon rolls."

"If you don't mind I'll sleep in until they get back," I said walking to my room with Josh and Harley's support.

"Harley, I can make up the couch for you," Mom said following us.

"That's okay. I can sleep in Kerry's room on the floor. Maybe Shadow will share his bed."

"*Don't press your luck.*" Harley and I heard Shadow snort.

"*Just kidding Shadow*," Harley said and we both smiled. Josh let go my arm as Harley, and I entered my room.

"I'm going to stay up a while," Josh said. "If I help Danene get the Christmas decorations out, perhaps she will go with us to cut the tree."

I grinned at Harley. Not surprised that Josh would find an opportunity to spend time with Danene. Their last meeting they seemed quite taken with each other.

"Shadow, have you heard from Brother Wolf," I asked sitting down on my bed. "I worry about him in this cold when I know he hasn't regained his strength any more than we have."

"*He and his mate are under a large blue spruce past the milk barn.*"

"Kerry, I will see if your mom has another roast I can take out to them. Another couple of days I think they

51

will be able to hunt for themselves. Your wounds are healing well. A now most of the stress is off your shoulders, rest is what you need." Harley opened the door, and Nakiya was standing in the doorway with two blankets and a pillow.

"Sally gave these to me to give to you, Harley," she said looking over at me. "Can I talk to you Kerry?" She asked walking into the room. "Where do you want me to put these?"

"Sure," I said trying to control the flip-flops in my stomach. "You can put them on Josh's bed. I need to get the sleeping mat out of my closet before Harley can make up his bed."

"Where's it at and I can get it out for you," she offered walking over to the closet.

"It's to your left in a green and blue box after the row of hunting gear." Nakiya returned with the matt and set it on top of the bedding she had brought in.

"Kerry, I can tell your anger with me for my decision to marry Dark Antelope. You haven't said two words to me since you returned," she said looking at the pictures on the wall. "I didn't have a choice, you know. Sometimes we have to put others ahead of ourselves. My feelings for you haven't changed."

I could not tell her I knew the reason she was forced to marry Dark Antelope. My brain scrambled looking for something to say. There was no help from Moon Dancer as he had gone back to sleep.

"You and Moon Dancer think this Shawgun wants me for a blood sacrifice. However, I think you are both wrong. Even if it were so, here I am protected, and when married to Dark Antelope, he will protect me. He would never let anything happen to me. Even as children he has watched over me."

There was no chance of talking Nakiya out of her decision. When a woman thought she was right, forget it. I had learned that from my mom and sister. More from my sister once she had her mind set on something.

"I don't know what to say then, Nakiya. You have made up your mind. I'm just glad you decided to spend Christmas with us. Christmas eve afternoon the family goes into town to participate in the celebrations," I said pulling my covers back on my bed. "You should go in with them." I wanted to talk her out of her decision and hold her in my arms, but I held my ground. Nakiya, I'm tired."

"Okay. I thought we could talk a while, but I guess I was wrong. I am sorry Kerry I will leave. Goodnight," she said her eyes cast down she closed the door behind her when she left.

"*You did the right thing, Kerry,*" Shadow said. "*Now get some sleep.*"

I slid into my bed, my heart heavy. Tears blanketed my cheeks, as I knew very well that I had to think of others and not my feelings for Nakiya. She must think my feelings for her had changed, which was the furthest thing from the truth. I loved her.

CHAPTER 4

"Spirit Walker wake up and come with me."

"Night Eagle, where are we going?" I asked as my spirit left my body. Josh and Harley were asleep so I assumed it must be in the early morning hours. Drifting out into the night, I saw Night Eagle perched on a leafless Aspen branch.

"Come our time is short, Spirit Walker." Deeper into Montana's majestic mountains I followed him. Their raw beauty still untouched in many areas by humans. The stars and the moon still a week from being full, illuminated snow covered sentinels guarding the Cabinets. The heavy snowfall would reach belly deep on a horse, leaving us the only option of snowshoeing.

"The gorge I've foreseen has a faulty crossing. The timber beneath the snow is old and decayed. With the weight of the snow and the weight of a human, the bridge could collapse several places. Shawgun may take advantage setting a trap forcing you to cross here. Falling into the gorge would stop you from reaching the place where Moon Dancer's third gift rest. I have suspected he is using other minions to stop you and Moon Dancer. The closer the moon comes to be blood red, Shawgun will find ways to increase his power," Night Eagle said and swooped closer to the gorge.

Following him, I remembered, *"The other place to cross is up a quarter mile. Snowshoe Lake is at the base of Snowshoe Peak and will be frozen over by now. Is this where you see Shawgun hiding?"*

"The pull of evil is stronger around Snowshoe Peak this end of the Cabinets. He cannot hide all his taint, but even I cannot pinpoint where he is hiding exactly. Come, it is time to go back." Night Eagle and I turned back passing in front of the rock face. I scanned the high rocky mountain range. Snowshoe Peak was not a high elevation as some. However, it was still difficult to reach.

My body was resting peacefully when I reentered. I heard the soft snores of my three companions and smiled. I'd never had close friendships other than Shadow and Mya. However, I knew my friendship with Josh and Harley would last a lifetime.

Laughter woke me up. I suspected they had returned from cutting the Christmas tree. Looking around my room, I was the only one left. Josh made his bed, and Harley had put his bed makings in the closet. Shadow had left the room, also. I imagined he would be with Nakiya. I sat up feeling stronger. Stretching my muscles to get my blood flowing I felt a new energy. The aroma of cinnamon rolls teased my nostrils.

"Good you're up," Mom said standing in the doorway. "Everyone has eaten. Do you want waffles with your bacon and eggs?"

"That sounds great, Mom. You made cinnamon rolls I could smell them from my room. Did Nakiya help you?"

"She did. She stayed here when they went to cut the tree. They are getting ready to decorate it. Are you going to help?" she asked.

"No. I may watch but I have to go through the photos that I took at the campsite and reference them to Harley's father's information," I said putting on my robe.

"You'll be able to counteract Shawgun's spells, with this?"

I was not the one who could interpret or who could read the Southwest Indians symbols. That would have to be Harley, Nakiya or Josh. Reversing Shawgun's curse I am sure was like learning another tribe's language. Like me learning another countries language.

"Somehow I have to, Mom," I said picking up my clothes. "Do I have time to take a shower before I eat?"

"Yes. I'll go start the bacon." She had brushed a kiss across my cheek before she left my room.

Walking into the family room, tree decorating was in full swing. Steve and Danene had finished putting on the usual five strands of lights. Ornaments spread everywhere waited attention. I cautiously maneuvered my way to the kitchen. Danene and Josh were stringing popcorn having their conversation. Dad was standing on a step stool putting the star atop the eight-foot tree while my brothers were picking out their favorite ornaments.

Nakiya, sitting at the counter her bare toes rubbing across Shadows back while he slept played with the marshmallows in her hot chocolate. Harley stood at the end of the counter with a big smile on his face. His fingers covered with icing from a hot cinnamon roll.

"I see where your loyalties lay, Shadow."

He opened one eye, *"I'm keeping watch over her so you can concentrate on the things that are most important."* I shook my head and smiled. Harley chuckled.

"You got a girlfriend Harley?" I asked.

"Nope. Haven't time for such foolishness." He continued licking the frosting from his fingers.

"I hope I'm around when that special girl brings you to your knees," I said.

His response a chuckle, *"You're going to have a long wait."*

"Good morning," I said sliding into a chair at the counter.

"How are you feeling?" Nakiya asked licking the marshmallow off her spoon. "It's closer to noon."

By the tone of her voice, I was not sure if it was sarcasm she dished out until I seen the corners of her mouth crescent, she was kidding with me. "Considerably better than last night," I replied. Mom set a plate of bacon n eggs, hash browns and a side dish of golden brown waffles in front of me. "Thanks, Mom," My stomach growled. I spread ketchup over my hash browns and mixed them together just as I like. Quickly putting a forkful in my mouth, not wanting to answer any more questions, but knowing I could only put it off so long, when Steve sat down beside me.

"There were wolf tracks around the outer carrels early this morning. I didn't follow them as they went back into the tree line," Steve said rubbing his left hand over his right. "I've told the others. No one goes out without a gun or alone."

"Harley, have you talked to Brother Wolf this morning?"

"Yes. He said they were not from his pack. He and his mate would be going back to their pack today."

"Jace, do you think if I was to get hurt again that it would affect Shadow and Brother Wolf?"

"Kerry I'm not sure, but I wouldn't count it out," Jace said continuing into the kitchen. "I've never encountered anything like that before."

Understanding Jace's hesitations, I nodded my head then I turned my attention to Rob and Dad's conversation.

"Today, three clients are picking up their horses. I do not want to take a chance on losing them to Kerry's demon. I've told them if they weren't satisfied with the training, they can bring them back next spring," Rob stated.

"That was a good idea," Dad countered.

"Are you going to feel up to going into town for the Christmas program?" Rob asked me.

"I think I will pass this year. They'll just have one less McDaniels singing," I said. "I encouraged Nakiya to go in with you."

"Maybe we should all pass this year," Steve remarked. "We could say we all come down with something.

"I can't remember a Christmas celebration that the family hasn't sung. We're as much a tradition as the Christmas parade in town," I stated. "It's only for a couple of hours. I will be fine here.

"Josh and I are staying with you. We have a lot to do," Harley replied and finished his roll.

"Nakiya you'll have fun," Danene said excitedly and burst into song, Rest Ye Merry Gentlemen.

Of course, the family joined her.

After the Rob's clients picked up their horses, we put the rest of the riding stock inside the riding arena. The two steers in a small enclosure at the south end. It was the first time I had been outside since they brought me into the house from the vet hospital. The fresh air filled my lungs passing the oxygen into the rest of my body. Taking things for granted, I would never do that again. I looked for Brother Wolf and his mate and found the area under a large pine empty.

Harley and I checked around the outside of the house for footprints, human or animal. There were no new ones.

"Night Eagle thinks Shawgun will try again before we seek him out. What do you think, Harley?"

"I think he will, only because he knows you grow stronger as he grows weaker. How is Moon Dancer?"

"He sleeps a lot to conserve his energy. I know he grows weaker as well," I said. "Do you know if I lose Moon Dancer before we separate, will I die."

"That is something he would be able to answer better than me. Have you asked your spirit animal, White Wolf?"

"No. I suspect I'm afraid of the answer I'd get."

"Remember Kerry, knowledge is power only if you use it. Haven't you felt powerless through most of this adventure?" Harley asked stomping the snow from his boots.

"I have. I've let my emotions control me and surprised I'm still alive right now." After hanging my coat on the horse head hook, I sat on the bench underneath it and slid my boots off. "We need to look over the pictures from the campsite tonight. If what Mr. Chavez said is true the book will give us the knowledge to destroy Shawgun. Which of the three of you know the southwest tribes symbols?"

"I don't Kerry." Harley placed his boots by the door hung his coat above them the butt of the gun inside his boot the stock covered by his coat.

"You fixing for a fast get away, Harley?"

He smiled while placing the shells to the gun in his coat pocket. I put the safety on my gun before putting it in the case.

It was only a minute or so before Josh came inside. The expression on his face had me concerned. What had he found that we had missed? I watched him secure his rifle and set it in the case next to mine.

"What did you find, Josh?" Harley and I stood in our stocking feet feeling the cold creep in waiting for Josh to take his gear off. I knew why he lingered when Mom stepped into the mudroom with a mop.

"We don't need that melted snow tracking into the kitchen," she said swooshing it back and forth several times before. When she finished, she set the mop inside the bucket by the door.

Josh turned his back to the inner doorway and lowered his voice when he spoke. "On the east side I found bear tracks. I am hoping they are not new ones. The tracks, came out of the timberline however, nothing went back. It's like they vanished."

"I believe the animals are safe. The riding arena is well built for heavy snowfall," I said trying not to shiver. "I'll talk to Steve about it." We ventured back into the warmth of the house.

"Josh do you know any of the southwest Indian symbols," I asked.

"That would be Nakiya. She is quiet knowledgeable about many tribes as she studied them in school."

My heart wrenched. I was trying to keep my distance from Nakiya. Proximity to her was defiantly going to test me. A wave of dizziness hit me.

"Kerry you alright," Josh asked. "You've paled. I think you need to rest before you do anything else today."

"I'll be okay. Just need to rest for a few minutes. The fresh air did me good." Josh's brow crunched as he looked at me. "Really. A few hours rest I'll feel like a spring chicken."

Harley rolled his eyes and laughed.

I scowled at him "Well, maybe not a spring chicken, however a short rest will make a big difference."

Entering the kitchen Mom, Danene and Nakiya were busy. On the counter set, three apple pies and the table decorated in Christmas decor. Danene was mashing potatoes humming a Christmas song when then the scene was spoiled by three quick gunshots. A signal someone was in trouble. Josh and Harley sprinted back to the mudroom and rapidly put on their coats and boots.

"Kerry you stay here with the girls." Harley, his gun in hand was inserting shells. Josh took his gun out of the rifle cabinet, and they were out the door before I could object.

"Shadow what is going on?"

"I'm not sure. I am at the other end of the yard. I see Poncho pulling the wood sled at a run coming from river road. Your dad is at the reins, and Rob is riding his horse following up the rear."

"Do you see my other brothers?"

"Jace went on a vet call about an hour ago. I do not see Steve. They are coming into the yard now. Looks like they stopped at the hospital."

"What's going on, Kerry?" Mom asked wiping her hands on a towel.

"I'm not sure. Stay here," I urged. I dressed quickly not bothering to lace up my boots all the way. Taking my gun from the gun cabinet, I went out the door as fast as my leg would allow. Dad and Rob were carrying Steve into the vet hospital followed by Harley and Josh.

When I hobbled in, they were cutting Steve's bloody jacket off. There was blood coming from a head wound.

"What happened," I yelled moving closer but stayed out of the way.

"We were bringing the wood supply down from another camp. A grizzly came out of nowhere, took Steve's horse down and ripped into him before we could get off a shot. We had wounded the darn thing before it ran up into the thicker pine trees. We did not go after it with Steve bleeding like this. We had to shoot Steve's horse."

"Where's Jace?" Rob yelled.

"He was called by one of the ranchers and left about an hour ago," I answered.

"Rob, bring me some hot water and clean towels," Josh said calmly putting his hand on Rob's arm.

"What's going on Spirit Walker?"

"Moon Dancer, I think Shawgun attacked my brother. They had to put the horse down. Josh is assessing Steve's injuries now."

"This is not good. Shawgun is finding ways to strengthen him. Taking the life force energy from the horse and anything else he kills."

Rob did not give Josh a second look before he went to do what he asked. I fired up the pot-bellied stove and retrieved the extra blankets from the supply case.

"Harley," Josh said. "Go to Kerry's room and get my bag with the herbs."

Harley left before Josh finished his sentence. "Kerry, help us get this blanket under Steve."

Rolling him onto his side, Rob and I pushed the blanket under Steve's back and then rolled him toward us. Dad pulled the remaining blanket towards him. With Steve's shirt removed, we could see where the bear claw came across his chest.

"I'm more worried about his head wound than I am his chest. Three claw rakes aren't that deep thanks to his winter clothing he had on," Josh commented.

Rob set the hot water on a stool next to the table. Rung the water out of the washcloth and started removing the blood. Josh examined Steve's head. Harley returned with the women trailing right behind him. He just shrugged his shoulders when he entered the room.

"What happened, Jacob?" Mom cried looking down at her second born son."

"A grizzly took Steve and his horse down and then preceded to open the horse's underbelly. We had to shoot him."

"Don't worry Sally. Only one claw rake is deep, but it is not life threatening. I will let Harley care for them. He did a great job on Kerry's." Josh commented.

Rob set more hot water on another stool next to the table along with clean cloths. Harley without saying a word went to work cleaning the claw rakes. One rake would need stitches the other two taped. Mom realizing stitches were in order, gathered the necessary things, and placed them on the tray. She wheeled it over next to Harley.

Josh patted blood away, until he could discover the proximity of the actual wound on Steve's head. "The bleeding has stopped," Josh said. "I'll have to wait until Harley's is finished stitching his chest. The skin break across the back of his head cannot be tended until we turn him. I am worried about the possibility of a concussion. He must have taken a hard blow to the head, for him still to be out. A blessing right now, until Harley finishes stitching him up.

"Rob, bring our rifles in here," Dad said. "And would you take Steve's saddle to the tack room, also?"

"You stayed to get his gear?" Danene asked shaking her head.

"Sis, when his horse fell, it pinned him underneath his shoulder. You should check his right leg, hope it's not broke," Rob said opening the door to go out.

"Alright girls, looks like Steve is in good hands here. Let's go back to the house and finish getting supper," Mom concluded.

I knew she did not want to leave. However, we were not little boys anymore, and we needed to get the rest of Steve's clothes removed. Josh checked his leg. A large bruise was already forming the bone intact. The claw rake on the back of his head was wide but not deep. Harley's salve would have it healed in no time.

"What will Steve say about the shaved strip I'm going to make across the back of his head?" Harley asked grinning.

A half hour later, we heard Steve groan. Harley was finishing up with the poultice wrap.

"It's alright son," Dad said with his hand on Steve's arm. Don't try and get up yet."

"What happened?" Steve asked his face sequenced in pain. He felt across his chest feeling the bandage.

Harley smiled as Harley always does. "I'll need to change this twice a day. I don't want those wounds to get infected," he said.

Steve just nodded.

Dad related the story of what happened and after helped him into a pair of sweats Rob had brought out and the flannel shirt.

"This wasn't supposed to happen. Shawgun has never bothered my family before."

"He's getting desperate, Spirit Walker. He has always been able to go between Earth and Icebis to generate his power." Moon Dancer said and continued. "Now he has to find other ways to accomplish this."

"Dad said they wounded the grizzly, will that not weaken him more?"

"Not knowing the extent of his injury, I don't know. The only thing in your favor now is he has lost a demon and had another wounded. I would not think he would attempt anything else here at the ranch. The danger is too great for him.

CHAPTER 5

I ventured into Steve's room. He was not sleeping though his eyes were shut. After pulling the rocker closer to his bed, I sat down. His eyelids lifted slightly and then closed again.

"Bro, I'm sorry I brought this upon us. I've done everything possible to keep Shawgun away from the family." Sighing, my eyes downcast, they followed the design in the carpet before looking back at my brother.

Steve opened his eyes, looked over at me saying nothing for a few moments.

"Listening to Josh tell it, you had no choice Kerry. I can't begrudge my little brother for something he had no control over." Trying to sit up, he caught his breath as pain washes across his face. "Promise me you won't hold anything else back that's happening to you."

My head hung down. How could I make that promise and not lie to him again?

"Kerry, what are you holding back? Something, it's written all over your face, and your skin looks the color of Mom's pink roses after they have been in the vase for a week.

"Steve, I don't know if you can handle what I haven't told you. Do you have a strong heart? Scaring you besides causing you more pain isn't on my agenda today."

He looked at me for another long moment. By the look in his eyes, he was considering me telling him what it was I was still hiding, or let it go. He gently ran his hand across his chest and in that instant, I knew. I scanned the room for any weapons.

"What's your favorite small animal? I ask, knowing there was not room in here for a Stag.

"My what? What does that have to do with anything?" He asked surprised.

"What's your favorite small animal or bird? Just tell me." His look changed to suspicion, drawing his eyebrows together and the dimple in his chin deepened slightly.

"Eagle, I suppose would be my favorite bird."

Not wanting to scratch the large end-board of Steve's bed, I picked up a throw rug and spread it over the wood.

"Moon Dancer I'm going to shape-shift so wake up. I can't lie to Steve anymore."

Moon Dancer shifted in my mind. He was awakening. Taking a big breath and concentrating on the eagle seen flying over Strawberry Meadows during the summer, I shape- shifted. I heard Steve's quick breath

71

intake as I latched on to the end board of his bed. My wings settled against my body. We stared at each other.

"This isn't a trick? It's you inside that Eagle?" He asked his hands fisted full of bed coverings. Then I heard him yell for Rob.

Rob quickly came through the open door, "What's the matter Steve?" He stopped in his tracks. "How did that eagle get in here?"

"Never mind how he got in here. Please get the family. Calmly, I don't want to scare him."

Rob left. I sat on the end board unable to speak to Steve. I hoped that when Rob came back that Harley would come with them. Shadow peered inside the room.

"Shadow, go bring Harley in here?"

Shadow and Harley returned before the family. *"Harley, tell Steve thanks for not panicking when I shifted."*

"Kerry says thanks for not panicking when he shifted."

"You can talk to him when he's in that form?" Steve asked trying to sit up a bit more.

"Here let me help you. You don't want to pull any of those stitches I put in you," Harley said putting another pillow behind Steve and helping him into a better sitting position. Finished, Harley came over and stood by me. We could hear fast footsteps coming down the hall. The door flew open that Harley had closed. Everyone flooded into the room. They all stood in shock except Jace.

"Are you alright, son," Dad asked looking at the large eagle perched on the bed.

"Yes, I'm fine. I want to introduce you to another one of Kerry's secrets he has kept from us."

I recoiled hearing it put that way.

"What are you talking about and how did that eagle get in here?" Rob asked again.

"Kerry, is that something you had to do now?" Jace asks shaking his head.

"Kerry says yes. Steve made him promise not to keep any more secrets from the family," Harley said repeating what Kerry told him.

Jace nodded his head. "You can shape-shift back. They will all believe you now."

"Shape-shift," Danene spit out, "Are you kidding me?"

My wings fluttered, and seconds later I was sitting on the end of Steve's bed. I heard them all gasp. Silence struck again.

"I don't even want to know." Were the first words out on my dad's mouth.

Rob sat down in the rocker, "How is this possible!"

Danene leaned up against the wall for support. "Are you kidding me?"

Mom put her arms around me and started crying. Josh and Nakiya come in wondering what all the commotion was about.

"Kerry shape-shifted," Harley said to them.

"Is this also part of the legend?" Dad asked looking back at Josh.

"No sir. That happened by accident. And since I wasn't there, Kerry would have to tell you how it happened."

All eyes turned back to me. I defiantly was not going to tell them about traveling to the planet Icebis. That could be told another time if need be. Not a lie if I omitted that bit of information for the time being.

"It happened when we found the second gift of Moon Dancers. The blue Orb was the size of a walnut. Trying to get away, I did not have any place to put the thing, so I popped it into my mouth. In the heat of things, I swallowed it. That started my shape-shifting."

"That was a concise statement," Moon Dancer stated. *"Well done."*

Shadow came over and stood by me. I put my hand inside his fur and felt his calm enter my body. I took a deep breath and let it out slowly.

"Is that all the secrets you've been holding on to Kerry?" Steve asked.

I looked around the room and sighed. "Yes. The visions and the dream walking you can ask about later. That is all the secrets."

"Can you change into any animal, Kerry?" Danene asked after the initial shock.

Danene, of course, would look at the bigger picture.

"This ability is to be a family secret. It's not something to exploit Sis to get more clients to come to the ranch," I said sternly. "So forget it. I can see the dollar signs in your eyes. This ability is sacred and used for one thing and one thing only, my taxidermy. Well, and maybe to help eliminate the demon Shawgun.

"I just come from Anderson's ranch. He lost two cows, and told me the ranch over from him lost another prize bull," Jace stated. He glanced around the room at all of us. "The cows at Anderson's were killed by a bear, so I'm assuming the bull was killed the some way. We do not want anything that Kerry can do out of the ordinary spoken of outside this house.

"But I haven't dreamed! How can that be?" I spoke to Moon Dancer

"No, you haven't Spirit Walker. Shawgun is building power. With kills, he takes their life force. He is preparing to do battle with us. We have to get the reverse for the curse translated from the book Mr. Chavez gave you."

"I agree," my father said. "I want your word of honor as McDaniels none of you will ever talk about Kerry's ability to shape-shift outside this house, or anyone other than a family member. Do I have your promise? Josh, Nakiya and Harley I would like your word also though I probably don't need it, I'd like to hear it anyway."

The only one that showed the slightest hesitation was Danene. However, I knew if she gave her word it was good as gold.

"I called the Mayor and told him we wouldn't be in for the Christmas Eve celebration because some of us were sick," Dad said. "The less explaining I have to do the better and since Doc wasn't called out for Steve, no one will be the wiser. However, that doesn't mean we can't have our celebration here."

"Sorry Nakiya, you would have enjoyed the performances in town," I say.

"That's alright Kerry. Josh said it would be better that we stay together. Your mom, Danene and I have made some special treats for tonight," Nakiya replied. "This will still be a special Christmas Eve," she said giving my hand a squeeze.

My heart fluttered at her touch and the thought of Dark Antelope holding… no, I cannot think of that. I have to focus on my mission. I released her hand and walked down the hall to Steve's room. I knocked once and entered. Steve is dressed and making his bed.

"How are you feeling?" I ask putting the rocker back in its place by the window.

"Like a bear has clawed me. How'd you think I'd be feeling," he said placing the pillows against the headboard.

"I'm sorry Steve. I tried hard to protect you all." Slumping into the rocker, I gazed out the window. It was snowing again. The trees laced in white reflected the colors across the few trees the family had decorated with lights. "I'm sorry about your horse, too."

"How's the leg," he asked in return changing the subject.

"It's doing much better. Harley has a real knack for healing, as does Josh. I've just had more healing experiences with Harley."

"And when are you supposed to go after that demon?"

"When the snow sticks to the rock face of the Cabinets near Snowshoe Peak is what White Wolf has told me."

"Is that the wolf we helped?" Steve asked opening up the chest at the foot of his bed.

"No. That was Brother Wolf. White Wolf is one of my spirit guides. He was the first to come to me in the cave."

"I've never let anyone use these," he said pulling out the two-gunned holster.

The pistols I had only seen a couple of times before when Steve had taken them out to clean. They had been our grandfather's and I knew by the way Steve took care of them they meant a lot to him.

"If you think you can use them, you can take them with you," he said running his fingers reverently over the pistols.

"I appreciate that. However, I don't think it will be a gun that will be Shawgun's demise."

"Kerry, I can't wrap my head around any of this, and if I hadn't seen with my own two eyes what I've seen, I'd still say you had a pipedream," he said putting the guns back in the chest and closing the lid. "I need to know how to help you, little brother."

"Believe in me. Sometimes, I have a hard time believing in myself. I have blunder things up, coming close to getting Shadow and I killed. I have to stay focused, and that's hard to do with Nakiya here."

"I can understand that. She's a pretty little filly," he said rubbing his hand across a three-day growth on his face. "I'll support you even if it kills me watching you trek up that mountain without us. I don't have to like it though."

"Thanks, Bro. That is all I ask."

Everyone was sitting in the family room waiting for Dad to turn on the Christmas tree lights. I could smell hot Wassail mingled with other scrupulous aromas. Under the tree, as if by magic because I had not seen them earlier in the day, were presents all shapes and sizes. I sat on the floor letting Shadow lie down beside me on one side, and Harley sat down on the other. I was surprised to see him in his Blackfeet traditional clothing. Looking over at Jace sitting next to Josh, my eyes lit up seeing Josh and Nakiya dressed in theirs.

Dad stood up with a mug of Wassail in his hand watching Mom and Danene give a glass to each of us.

"This year has been one with mixed blessing. The ranch has prospered. Rob has sold almost twice as many horses than last year. Our commodities have brought a good price, and the herd has expanded. We did six more river trips and five more hunts. We have made new friends. Kerry has found new skills," he said and gave a little cough. "We need to thank God and, as our new friends say The Great Spirit for the blessings we've received this year. We ask him to keep you safe Kerry," Dad said raising his cup toward me. "And this mission you are on which frankly I don't understand, but be as it may, that you will accomplish it and return safely to us. Cheers."

My eyes filled with tears. Putting my hand on Shadow's back, I quickly rescued my composure. "Thanks, Dad," I say raising my cup to him before I took a drink.

"Josh, Nakiya and Harley are going to show us a few of their traditions before we open the presents," Mom said sitting down beside my dad.

Josh played the small drum and Harley and Nakiya danced. We even joined in with Harley trying to follow along. We were enjoying the second number when Shadow jumped up and launched to the French doors.

"Kerry, evil is outside the house. Some are trying to get inside the riding area."

"What kind of animals?"

"I sense wolves. Not sure the number around the house."

"Did you hear that Harley?" Harley stopped dancing.

"Dad we have wolves around the house and some are trying to get inside the riding area."

"Steve you stay inside this house and protect your mom and the girls," Dad yelled, opening the gun case in the family room, he tossed Steve a rifle. Steve nodded catching the gun. Dad gave one to Mom, Danene and Nakiya.

We quickly put on our winter gear and checked our guns. Each of us put ammo in our pockets. Rob braced himself before Dad opened the door just in case one was that close. We heard glass breaking and gunshots come from the family room.

Jace ran back firing at the third wolf attempting entry through the shattered door. It fell over the tip of the Christmas tree now lying on its side. Two more attempted entry falling to our bullets crashing over wrapped gifts tearing the elegant bows and wrappings beyond repair. The Christmas lights flicked and went out. Popcorn and ornaments were everywhere but on the tree. The star, a family heirloom lay in pieces.

Harley and I raced to my bedroom. Opened the window looking for demon wolves that could be at this end of the house. There were tracks. The large glass doors must have looked like an easier entry than my small window.

"Steve, help me push the gun cabinet in front of the shattered door," Jace shouted. "Mom, keep that gun aimed at the door. Danene and Nakiya watch the front window."

We heard gunfire closer to the riding area. Climbing out the window Harley followed me out pushing the window closed after. Circling around we saw two more dead wolves by the kitchen door. Dad, Rob and Josh were racing to the riding area.

"Behind you, hit the ground Josh." My aim was straight and true taking down the wolf in midair. Josh jumped back up and continued after my dad and brother. We circled around the other way. Hearing more shots, we slowed, easing our way around the end of the structure. Four more wolves lay limply in the snow. A fifth struggled for the tree line. I took aim and fired. I was not sure if I hit him when another shot sounded from the house.

"Dad, you okay," I shouted putting my gun up to take aim again as I rounded the corner.

"Yah. They did not get in. Let's get back to the house."

"Go ahead. Harley and I will stay here just in case there are more," Josh yelled back.

I shuffled to catch up with Rob and Dad following them around to the shattered doors to the family room.

"Coming in," Dad shouted and then stepped through the space. The gun cabinet covered only one door. "You all right?"

"We're okay. Let's get these filthy animals out of here," Steve remarked.

"We'll do that Steve. Is that your blood on your shirt or theirs?" I asked.

"Darn if I know at this point."

It was still. "Shadow do you sense anymore?" speaking aloud I asked.

"*No Kerry.*"

Danene come back into the room carrying the broom and dustpan her gun still clutched under her arm. Glass was everywhere. Nakiya was picking up ripped packages and shaking them to remove the glass.

"Mom, are you okay?" I took the rifle from her setting it on the dining table.

"Look at my house," she cried pushing her red tangles off her face. "Is Josh and Harley okay?" She asked looking around the room.

"Yes. They stayed outside in case there were any stragglers. Shadow says if there were any left they've gone."

"Kerry, you and Rob go get a piece of plywood to cover the doors. Jace and I will start taking out these dead animals. I am sure Josh has a place to burn them. I did not see any that had yellow eyes. What a shame that demon infected them."

Hauling the plywood back, we saw where Josh had started to pile the dead wolves. We continued, it was too cold and we were losing heat in the house.

Nailing the plywood in place went quickly. The girls had the majority of glass swept and put in the garbage. Mom came from the utility closet with the vacuum. We left the girls to finish cleaning inside and went back to haul the wolves shot at the riding area. Counting 13, I listened to Josh sing around the circle of demon-possessed animals.

Lighting the torch he laid it to the pile watching it catch on fire. As before, we heard the terrible shriek come down the mountain. It lasted longer this time and chills ran up and down my spine. How was I going to conquer this abomination?

Everyone went inside with the exception of Josh and Harley. I could not hear what they were saying, but I got the jest that they were going to put a protection prayer around the house. Something we should have thought of earlier. What was done was done. A blessing could be a deterrent.

Chapter 6

"Kerry, Harley told me you need help with the southwest tribe symbols. I can help you translate the information that Mr. Chavez gave you," Nakiya said taking hold of my hand.

My blood ran hot at her touch. Looking into the depth of her dark chocolate eyes I lost myself. Putting a screeching halt to my feelings, I took back my hand and looked away.

"Yes, I do need help, Nakiya. Waiting any longer not an option. Shawgun has threatened my family. I had to translate that information before he could restore his full power. I'll be right back." I went to my room to gather the pictures I had taken at the campsite and the book Mr. Chavez had given me. Looking in my bedroom window was White Wolf and sitting on my windowsill was Night Eagle. I made haste to open it.

"*Spirit Walker your time frame to destroy Shawgun has shortened,*" White Wolf said.

"*Couldn't you have warned me about the attack last night,*" I screeched. "*Someone in my family could have been killed and my friends.*"

"*We can't foresee everything Spirit Walker. Calm down. Last night is past,*" Night Eagle stated.

"You're right. I am sorry. He's never attacked my family before," I say itching around my leg wound. *"Nakiya is going to help me translate the signs in Mr. Chavez's book. I was getting it right now."*

"You have to find him before the full moon in five days," White Wolf said. *"He's finding more ways to increase his power. At the blood red moon, he will need a sacrifice to restore all his power. That will leave the claw around your neck useless to you. Through this ritual, he will be able to regrow his finger and leave this planet. The claw around your neck will be his weapon to kill you."*

I sank to the floor. Here, I thought things could not get any worse; the bottom dropped out from underneath me. The claw I have worn around my neck that kept Shawgun from killing me himself could be the very thing that could end my life. My heart pumped faster. No more, time to waste. I picked up the book and the pictures and went back to the dining room.

"Nakiya, I can't read the language in the book Mr. Chavez gave me, nor do I know the meaning of the symbols drawn," I say setting the book open in front of her. "I hope you can translate."

"Kerry do you have a notebook and a pencil?" Nakiya asked turning a page in the book.

"Here, Nakiya," Mom said handing both to her.

I pulled a chair out next to Nakiya and sat down. I tried ignoring my feelings when her scent of cedar and citrus surrounded me. It still mystified me how she could turn me to mush. I sat close enough to look at the book but far enough not to touch her.

"Kerry, give me time to read through the book. I don't want to make any mistakes that could happen if I don't read it all first."

"Oh, sure. Give me a yell when you're ready." I said. In the kitchen, I took out the peach cobbler and the whipping cream from the fridge. Food was a way of stuffing my feeling away. "Where is everyone?" I asked sitting up to the counter next to Mom.

"They went out to check things around the ranch. Surely, this isn't the Christmas I expected us to have," she stated tears misting her eyes. "I put the gifts in the storage closet. No one was in the mood to open any of them or had an interest to the ones that had been torn open in the scrimmage. So after this is finished, and you destroy Shawgun…" Sob sob. "How can a country boy of 19 defeat a demon?"

Tears, a steady stream down my mother's face, broke my heart. There were very few times growing up I had seen her cry. She had always had a strong belief in the Lord. The Great Spirit, White Wolf and the Blackfeet called him. Believing that things would turn out the way he wanted them. Have faith in the outcome you want, we were taught growing up. Right now, I needed all the faith I could muster.

"I'm sorry, Mom. I didn't expect any of this to happen."

"By the sounds of it sweetheart, you didn't have much choice in the matter did you. I have to have faith that the Lord will direct you in what you need to do. Such a heavy burden for one so young," she cried wiping her tears with her apron.

The mudroom door opened and Dad my brothers, Harley and Josh come in covered with snow. My stomach growled, and I started in on my peach cobbler. After talking to them, I might not have much of an appetite. I ate quickly and had it finished when they came into the kitchen.

"How are things out there?" I asked putting my plate in the sink.

"Right now, all is quiet. I heard it's supposed to snow most the night," Jace said. He picked up the coffee pot and filled it with water.

"Here let me do that, Jace," Mom said getting up from the counter. "I should have had it on the stove already. The ham will be done in half hour. Danene will you put the potatoes on?" She asked when my sister walked in.

"How is the translation going?" Rob asked looking over at Nakiya sitting at the table.

"She wanted to read the book from beginning to end, so she didn't miss- interpret anything."

"I would agree with her. You have enough to worry about without having the wrong information. Is there anything we can help with?" Rob asked.

I shook my head there was nothing they could do, but wait.

"Kerry would you and Nakiya take that into your father's study so we can set the table."

I picked up the pad, pencil and pictures and led the way to my dad's study. His study was larger than my room, with a smaller rock fireplace than the family room. I set the things I carried down on the large oak desk. Pushing the grate aside, I added wood to take the chill away in the room.

"You can sit in my dad's chair, Nakiya. Would you like something to drink," I ask and watch her scan the room. Dad had pictures hanging on the wall of him and many of his clients, some with game they had shot. On his desk were pictures of the family. Two dark leather brown chairs set in front of his desk and a matching leather couch shared the west wall with an elk horn floor lamp.

"Your father knows some important people," she said and sat down in his chair. "I should have this finished read by supper and a cup of coffee would be great.

We could both smell the coffee aroma filling the house along with the ham and homemade rolls. I left her to continue reading and ask Danene to take her a cup of coffee.

"Moon Dancer, are you awake?"

"I'm here Spirit Walker. I can feel your doubt," He says and pauses. *"We can do this. You have healed at a remarkable rate and tonight you will learn the symbols to send Shawgun back to Icebis. Ask Running Wolf/Josh if he has any of the magic rocks from the river. You will need them to write the symbols.*

Everyone was trying to act as if this was a happy Christmas day. To a stranger, they could have pulled it off. However, you could cut the tension with a knife when I entered the kitchen.

"How is she doing?" Steve asked limping into the family room. He pulled a leather stool closer to the chair, sat down and put his leg up.

"Nakiya said she would be done by dinner. After dinner, we will start working on the symbols. I added more wood to the fire and sat down on the hearth watching the flames lick over the new logs. "I only have five days to destroy Shawgun, bro. It will take me a day and a half to reach Snowshoe Peak more than likely with this new snowfall."

"And you say we can't go with you?" he asked leaning forward in the chair.

"I have to do this on my own. Josh and Harley are coming with me but only so far," I say turning around to face him. "I can feel Moon Dancer getting weaker and I'm scared. It would be worse for me if any of you were with me. My attention would lack the concentration on what I have to do worrying about the lot of you. Knowing you are here watching over the ranch and each other, I can make this happen. I have prayed to the Great Spirit to help me, and I can only trust that he will.

"Dinner is ready," Mom stated.

I watched Danene go down the hall to the study. I presumed she was asking Nakiya to come to dinner. Mom did have the traditional flare on the table. Christmas china, red and green cloth napkins, winter scene, etched goblets and a small gift-wrapped box with a bow set in front of each plate. Shawgun might have put a damper on Christmas Eve, but mother was not going to let him spoil Christmas day.

"We can start with the symbols after dinner, Kerry," Nakiya said walking into the dining room. "Oh my, Sally. Your table is beautiful. Kerry can you take a picture with all of us behind the table. I would like to have a picture to show my parents."

Before I took a step to get my camera, Shadow came down the hall carrying the case strap in his mouth.

"So you think this is a good idea, too," I ask him. Taking the case from him, I set up the tripod, attached the camera to the stand and arranged everyone. I placed Nakiya and Shadow in front of the table where I would also sit. I focused the camera put it on automatic and hurried to take my place.

I took a few. It was hard to get everyone smiling or them with their eyes all open. Somewhere in the bunch would be one that everyone liked, I hoped. I took my camera into the dark room to start the process of developing.

"Memories are always good. No matter what happens your parents will have this picture of all of you together and happy."

"I'm glad you're awake, Moon Dancer. We will all be together after this is over. We haven't come this far to fail now," I say.

"You're right. We haven't," Moon Dancer agreed. *Meaning we only have a few days left to accomplish our mission. A few days left until we separate. I will go home to Icebis and you will fulfill your destiny here.*

"Moon Dancer I promised Running Wolf I would ask you if he could talk to you before you leave." There was a pause. I pulled the film out of my camera while I waited for his answer.

"Not this night. This night you need to complete the sequence of symbols that we will use against Shawgun. I may be able to help you some. We need to reverse the curse, and listening to you, my great-great granddaughter, Nakiya will have a big part in this."

"We are going to work on it as soon as we eat and open the gift Mom and Dad bought each of us. She says the rest can wait until this is over.

"Your mother is wise," he said. "When you are ready, call me."

I just finished the film process when there was a knock on the door.

"Kerry, we're ready to eat," Jace said.

"I'll be right there." I hurried and cleaned up my work area. Five minutes later I was sitting at the table mother had so beautifully decorated. Another one of her talents and one she had passed on to Danene. As a tradition, Dad said the Christmas prayer.

The atmosphere was almost normal. Great food helped and the red wine we saved for special occasions wasn't bad either. Finishing the bread pudding with camel sauce, we talked about the last year's accomplishments, what went well and things we could improve. No one brought up the losses we had had due to my dreams. However, overall, Rose-Feather Ranch and Outfitters had a great year.

"You can open your presents now," Mom said sitting back in her chair, taking my dad's hand.

We all looked at each other.

"I'm not going to waste any more time," Danene said and tore the paper off the small box.

Opening the lid, she gasped. "It's beautiful," she said lifting the tiny gold chain from the box. On the chain was a rectangular locket etched with the ranches' Rose Feather emblem.

Nakiya opened hers next. The chain and locket were the same except etched the physician's symbol. Tears came to her eyes, and she forced back the sobs. I knew she thought after marrying Dark Antelope, she would never be able to go to medical school.

"It's beautiful. I do not know what to say. Thank you does not seem to be enough.

"You're welcome Nakiya. Dreams come true even when we lose hope for them," Mom said.

Wrapping flew as Harley opened his. A rectangular gold dog tag hung from a thicker gold chain.

"Harley, yours isn't etched. Since you were a surprise here for Christmas; and thank goodness, you came, we wanted you to have one also. You are a special young man to us. Decide what you want, and we'll have it etched after the holidays."

"Thank you," he said humbly and put the chain around his neck.

Steve and Jace opened theirs next. They were larger gold chains but instead of a locket, it resembled a gold dog tag also. Steve's etching was a Herford bull, while Jace's was the Veterinary symbol. Rob and Josh finally opened their small boxes. Theirs were the same as the other boys with the exception Rob's etching was of a horse and Josh had the veterinarian symbol. He graduated from vet school the end of summer.

"You're too kind," Josh said looking at my parents. "I thank you for your generosity."

"Aren't you going to open yours, Kerry?" Danene asked and threw her bow at me.

"Sure, I was enjoying watching all of you open yours," I say. Quickly removing the wrapping paper from my own small box. Etched on the gold dog tag was my Blackfeet name, Spirit Walker. 'Thanks, Mom and Dad. I'll always wear it." I felt a warming on my chest as it rested against my skin.

"I'm glad you like them. Jacob and I had long discussions deciding on what symbol to put on them.

"Nakiya and I need to work on Mr. Chavez's book in Dad's study if you need us for anything.

When we sat down at Dad's desk, it was 7: 13p.m... Shadow lay beside me. Nakiya had notes spread out over most the wood surface.

"These are the pictures from the camp site, Kerry. I tried to assemble them on these pieces of paper. We might want to ask Otter, (she used Harley's tribal name) if they look correct.

These symbols are the ones we will use to reverse the curse on Moon Dancer, separating the two of you and vanquishing Shawgun back to the dark side of Icebis. We'll use passages in the book to correlate with each symbol," she said continuing to look at the papers she had written.

The French doors blew open, sending papers scattering everywhere. I leaped to close the doors and lock them.

"Kerry in the fireplace," Nakiya yelled. Mr. Chavez's book is catching fire."

Chapter 7

I sprinted to the fireplace caught hold of the book's cover and pulled it onto the bricks in front of the fireplace. I stomped the flamed edges and watched the smoke rise. Smoke and Nakiya's scream brought the family into the room.

"What happened?" Jace spouted.

"The patio door flew open and the wind scattered everything off the desk and the book into the fireplace," I said

"I locked those doors myself, Kerry," Rob stated.

"I think we need to have someone with you at all times while you are working with that book," Josh said. "Is it still readable?"

"Let me look at it," Nakiya prompted.

I picked it up carefully trying not to smudge the pages and made sure the ambers were all out. I set it on the desk on a blank sheet of paper.

She turned the pages carefully. "I think I can finish."

I handed her my neckerchief to wipe the ash from her fingers. Picking up the pieces of paper off the floor that Nakiya had written on, we laid them back on the desk.

"We could do two hour shifts until they finish translating," Josh said checking the door again and pulling the curtains together.

"I think that would be a good idea." Dad said. "Josh, do you want to take the first swift?"

Mom did not wait for an answer when she asked.

"Josh, would you like some coffee or hot chocolate?" Wiping her hands on her apron as she had been frosting cookies.

"Hot chocolate would be nice," he said pulling the rocker closer to the doors.

"I'll get that for you," Danene stated and left the room. Shadow lay down beside Josh.

"I should be able to sense if evil tries to gain entrance again," Shadow mind spoke. We heard a wolf howl and I shivered.

"Is that more trouble," I asked Shadow

"No, that was Brother Wolf."

"Your right, I recognize his howl now. He is also keeping watch." I could feel my Spirit Animals close. *"Brother Wolf, thank you for coming. I do not wish to put you or your mate in harm's way."*

"My pack is here also. This demon has possessed many of our brethren. We will help you anyway we can, Spirit Walker."

Nakiya lined her notes and drawings in a row and carefully opened the burnt book to the page she had been working on.

"Half this page is gone, however I have the notes I need from this page," Nakiya said and sighed. "Kerry I will tell you which pieces of paper to separate as I go through this again. I am thinking not all my notes will be needed to break the spell. I'm just not sure which ones they are, yet."

"The four thunder spirits, these are regarded as powerful beings," she said and turned the page. "Oh, Kerry the paper figures."

"I didn't know you could draw, Nakiya," I say holding the paper up examining the drawing. "Josh, White Wolf asked if you have any of the magic rocks from the river?"

"I always carry one or two in my medicine bag. Why?"

Danene walked back into the room.

"I didn't know if you liked marshmallows in your hot chocolate or not so I put them on the plate," she said handing the plate to Josh. I looked at Nakiya and we smiled.

"Thanks Danene," he said standing up to take the plate from her.

"Well I best go help Mom." She walked out of the room her cheeks flushed. Josh was not the only one smitten.

I went back to the drawings when it hit me. "You don't except me to draw those on the cave wall, do you?" Drawing had never been of interest to me and since I could not draw a straight line…. "Can't I take pictures of the drawings and use them?"

"I'm not the one to ask, Kerry," Nakiya said looking up at me.

"I would consult your guides Kerry," Josh said and shrugged his shoulders. "Usually the strongest effect comes when the one doing the spell does it by hand."

My heart sunk looking at Nakiya's drawings.

I sat down in the corner, closed my eyes and called on Raven. Not since learning to shape-shift, had I talked to Raven. I had been so out of control, Raven put a spell on me so I could not use that gift until I learned to control it.

"Yes Spirit Walker, you have need of me?" Raven answered. He did not materialized but I felt him near me.

"Raven, the symbols that Nakiya is translating, will I need to draw them or will a picture do?" I asked.

"Spirit Walker you excel in photography. If you take each one individually, with nothing else in the photo, that will work. I will instruct you in the way to lay them out," Raven stated. *"I feel you hesitate. Scared things are not meant for all ears or eyes, Spirit Walker"*

"Okay, I understand."

"Shawgun is strong. Nakiya will be able to translate and draw the symbols. You will take the pictures and when they are processed, you are to wrap them in white paper, place them in an envelope and seal it closed. You still need the magic rock from Running Wolf/Josh. I will give you further instructions later. You have to find Shawguns hiding place and perform the ritual on the night of the blood red moon," Raven finished.

I had another question for Raven, but he was gone. I opened my eyes and took a deep breath. I looked around the room. I had not heard Jace come in. He was sitting in the other chair in front of Dad's desk.

"Nakiya needed drawing paper," he said.

"I had this feeling that I needed to draw these on plain paper, not lined. Did Raven answer you?" She asked putting the paper aside except for one, which she put in front of her to work on.

"Yes he gave me an answer. I can photograph them when you are finished," "Perhaps it was Raven that gave you the impulse to use the plain white paper."

101

She nodded, smiled, and went back to her drawing.

It was well after midnight, closer to 3a.m. I saw Nakiya's head nod. Harley was on watch at the window working on a leather pouch. Shadow lay next to Nakiya's chair. The house was silent, as everyone had gone to bed. I been studying the drawings Nakiya drew. The four Thunder Beings, powerful with lighting coming from their feet and hands, four female stick figures, two dark and two light representing good and evil. Father Sky and Mother Earth have a special energy. The body of Father Sky has the symbols of the moon, stars and sun, and the zigzag line meaning the connection to the Milky Way. I remember the Milky Way when I was taken to Icebis. I knew we were on the right track.

Nakiya's head nodded again.

"Nakiya, why don't you finish that later?" I ask taking the pencil from her hand and setting it on the desk.

"I only have one more to finish," she slurs and picks up the pencil.

I took it from her again and this time she looked up and smiled at me. "I guess you're right. I'll finish this when I wake up." She pushed the chair back and stood up her hands on her back. "Guess I'm a little stiff," she said rubbing the small of her back. "Good Night."

"I think you need sleep, too," Harley said looking up from his work.

"I do. I feel so overwhelmed Harley. Have you talked to your Father?"

"I have. He is concerned about the wolf attacks and the kills it takes to build his power. If not stopped the balance will falter. He says to listen to your spirit guides and do exactly as they say. He will say prayers for you."

"Thank him for me. Who will spell you?"

"Rob will be in at 4a.m... I'm fine. I took a nap this evening and I have Shadow to keep me company.

"Alright, I will see you later, good night Shadow."

I looked out my bedroom window. Right now, it looked peaceful. The almost full moon had a tinge of orange to it and the snow glistened under its brilliance. Josh's breathing was shallow. He was sleeping light and I think if I spoke to him, he would answer. Neither he nor anyone else could give me the answers I wanted. I knelt down beside my bed and prayed. Morning light would be here soon enough. One more drawing and we would be able to decipher the message to vanquish Shawgun and I would start my journey.

"Mom, did Nakiya come back in here?" Asked Danene.

"No I haven't seen her since the two of you went out to milk Daisy," Mom said, untying her apron. "Did you look inside the riding area? She might have gone in with your brothers. Jace and Josh went into town to get a few things and they should be back in an hour or so."

"I'll go look in the riding area."

"What are you looking for in the riding arena?" I asked sitting up to the counter.

"Nakiya. We went out to milk Daisy and when I returned with Daisy's hay Nakiya wasn't in the milk barn."

"I bet she's in the riding arena. I think she fell in love with Rosetta when she was here last summer," I said. "I would look there because I haven't seen her come back in the house and Harley is the only one in the study."

"I'm surprised because she was in a hurry to do that last drawing," Danene said picking up a cinnamon roll and then took a second and headed to the back door.

"You ready for breakfast? Harley said he'd wait to eat with you," Mom said putting her apron back on. "Will ham and eggs be okay this morning?"

"Mom whatever you want to fix, we'll eat," I said on my way back to the study. "Harley let's gather this all up and take it to the dining room table. Mom is fixing breakfast and I don't want to leave Nakiya's work in here."

We gathered everything up from the pencils to finished drawings and I put Mr. Chavez's book under my arm.

"You need to have this finished tonight. Tomorrow we have to leave if we are to make the Cabinets and find Shawguns hiding place before we run out of time," Harley said leading the way back to the kitchen.

"Night Eagle said it was near Snow Shoe Peak, and that is still a lot of area to search."

Danene came back in letting the screen door slam and tracking snow as she come into the kitchen.

"I can't find her," she said rubbing her hands together. I looked in the arena. Dad and Steve said they haven't seen her."

"Where's Shadow? He usually stays pretty close to her," I say. "

"Shadow where you at boy? Shadow, answer me." I strained but heard no reply. "Danene did Shadow go out with you this morning?"

"Yes. You know how he follows Nakiya everywhere."

"Shadow was with Nakiya in the milk barn?" My voice raising and my stomach started to knot. "You're sure they didn't go to town with Jace and her brother."

"I'm sure because they left before we went out to milk."

"Shadow, please answer me if you can hear me." Silence and more silence.

"Mom you and Danene stay in here and guard Nakiya's work on the table. Let's go see if we can find them, Harley. Maybe they just went for a walk.

"Wouldn't Shadow still answer you," Harley asked.

I gave him a serious look and he nodded. I did not want to get Mom upset. She turned back to the stove undoing her apron she laid it on the counter.

"I want a report in ten minutes or I'm going to be out there."

"No Mom. You have to stay with the drawings until we know what is going on. You too Danene and keep a rifle handy." Harley and I quickly put on our winter gear and picked up a rifle before going out the mudroom door.

"Let's go look in the riding arena and see if my dad and my brothers are still in there." Snow was starting to fall again. Just what we needed if we had to look for tracks. Dad and Rob were coming out of the arena.

"Have you seen Nakiya," I asked attempting to keep my voice even.

"No. Isn't she with Danene in the milk barn?" my dad asked.

"Danene can't find her and Shadow won't answer me."

"Let's go look in the milk barn again," Rob said turning and walked quickly in the other direction. We all quickened our steps and the closer to barn we could hear Daisy mooing. By the sound of it, she was not too happy they did not milk her.

We opened the milk barn door and Daisy turned around, eyed us and flipped her tail. We looked around her stall.

"Over here," Steve yelled from the back of the milk barn."

I gasped when I saw Shadow lying motionless in the straw. I see Steve reach down and feel his diaphragm.

"Is he still breathing?" I choked out.

"Yes. I'm not a vet but it feels like he has a good size goose egg and perhaps a concussion."

I pushed my way to him and knelt down beside him. *"Shadow talk to me boy. Shadow I'm here talk to me."* I felt him stir and his eyes snaked open and closed again. *"Shadow what happened? Where is Nakiya?* He lifted his head slightly.

"Dark Antelope." was all he said. I reached behind him and lifted him up. Harley secured his head stopping it from bobbing as we carried him to the vet hospital. "Rob,

can you look to see if Dark Antelope left any tracks? I knew if anyone could find a trace of Dark Antelope and Nakiya it would be Rob. His tracking ability was well known.

"Dark Antelope had to have used a spell to get past Brother Wolf and sneak up on Shadow," I say as Dad opened the door for us.

Steve put a blanket on the steel table and after started the potbelly stove.

"He could have shape-shift, we know he has done that before when you were learning to shape-shift yourself," Harley said.

"Spirit Walker get back to the house, danger," I heard Brother Wolf say urgently. "

"Dad, Steve, mom needs you back the house. Brother Wolf says there is danger." They picked up their rifles and scurried out. We heard a gunshot. I was torn, however, I stayed with Shadow. My feelings were being bounced around like a chicken with its head cut off.

"Kerry whatever is happening at the house your father and brother can handle. I've never dealt with this kind of injury before," Harley said. "I'm not sure what to do. I'm afraid he might have internal bleeding,"

Now I was terrified for Shadow and Nakiya. I closed my eyes and sent up a silent prayer. *We needed help! Great One, please send back Jace and Josh. Please keep*

Nakiya safe until I find her. I felt like I had an anvil pressing down on my shoulders, the weight leeching the strength I had manager to build back up from my injuries. This cannot be happening. Shadow could be dying, Nakiya was in the hands of Dark Antelope and the last drawing and the translation were not finished. I had put my family in danger giving into my feelings and letting my emotions take charge. I fought back the tears ready to escape my eyes. I had no time for tears. We needed to come up with a plan to put everything right. Not leaving in the morning to find Shawgun and Nakiya was not an option.

The door opened and Rob stepped into the room. "I hear the truck coming. They'll be here in just a few minutes," he said. I knew he was referring to Jace and Josh.

"I'm going to see what's happening at the house." Rob said and left before I could ask him what tracks he found, if any. I put a blanket over Shadow. His breathing was shallow, his eyes still shut. We had not heard any more shots from the house. I hope that that was a good sign.

The truck pulled up outside and I heard the truck doors open and shut the tailgate put down. Jace must have gone into town to replenish the supplies used. Harley went to the door and opened it. They both had their arms full.

"What is it?" Josh asked looking a Harley and then over at me. Then he saw Shadow on the table the same time Jace did.

"Dark Antelope was here," I began. "He took Nakiya and hit Shadow with something. He has a knot on his head. The only thing he said to me was, Dark Antelope. He hasn't opened his eyes again and his breathing scares me."

"And Nakiya? How did that happen?" Josh snorted, "Did any one try to follow them?"

"Rob was looking for tracks, but he ran back to the house before he told me what he'd found when we heard a gunshot come from that direction."

"Go talk to Rob, Josh. I will take care of Shadow. And send Steve out to update us on what happened in there, Jace said pulling the stool over to the table.

"I'm worried about concussion," Harley commented. "The skin wasn't broken, and as Kerry said he has quite a knot between his ears."

"He could have a concussion." Jace said feeling around Shadow's head. "And if that's the case only time will tell if he can pull out of it," Jace said lifting one of Shadows eyelids. "Kerry you haven't been able to mind speak with Shadow?"

"Like I said, Shadow said Dark Antelope and nothing since. Is he going to be all right Jace? I choked holding back the tears. Shadow had been my best friend since I was a small child. We had grown closer since we were able to mind speak. Losing him would be like losing a brother.

"I can't guarantee anything, Kerry. We'll just have to wait and monitor his breathing," Jace stated. "Did you and Nakiya finish the translation?

"No. she was up before I was this morning and Danene took her out with her to milk Daisy. Danene went to get hay for the cow and when she returned Nakiya was gone and Shadow was hidden in the straw on the other side of Daisy's stall.

"Brother Wolf wasn't alerted by his presences," Harley said.

"Brother Wolf did you recognize the evil?" I asked." Worried at the silence I called again. "Brother Wolf."

"I'm here Spirit Walker. It was a lone wolf from the other night. We chased him. He bleed out from a wound."

"Thank you Brother Wolf."

No one was hurt in the house. Rob and Josh went back out trying to pick up the trail of Dark Antelope and Nakiya. Snow was coming down in large flakes making it difficult to see. Nevertheless, I knew they would not return until they found them or the trail was completely covered up.

Dad and Mom passed by going out to feed the livestock, both were carrying rifles. So much had happened in a small amount of time. I sunk my hands into Shadow's coat. The calming effect I always counted on from him was missing.

CHAPTER 8

Jace sent me to the house. There was nothing I could do for Shadow. I needed the last drawing finished and then all of them translated into the sequence that would vanquish Shawgun. I stopped at the hitching post between the barn and the house and looked up toward the Cabinets. They were rugged when you reached the summit. Snow was sticking to the rock face and now too deep for a horse or pack mule. It would be snowshoes and a backpack, a challenge for the fittest hiker.

Danene was working on something at the table. I picked up a wood splinter and looking up, I noticed the bullet hole in the ceiling. I looked at it and then at Danene and she just shrugged.

"What happened? I asked.

"The jitters I guess. I thought I heard something at the window. I jumped and the rifle went off," she said. "I'm sorry if I scared you. How is Shadow?"

"Not good. Jace thinks he has a concussion, and there may be bleeding. We can only wait," I say.

"He's not a young pup anymore, Kerry. Animals are just like people as they age, they don't heal the way they did when they were younger."

"Don't put him in the grave," I say harshly.

"I'm sorry," she said and changed the subject. "You don't think that Dark Antelope will hurt Nakiya being they are betrothed and all?"

"She told you about that, huh."

"Frankly Danene, I don't think Dark Antelope knows what he is doing or why. I've never liked him, but on his own, no, I don't believe he would hurt her."

"Come look at this," Danene said and walked over to the dining room table where the drawings were laid out. "I've been playing around with this. I found a marker in the book and I think it was the last drawing Nakiya was working on."

I looked at the drawing and was stunned for a moment. "I didn't know that you could draw."

"Just because I couldn't take good photographs didn't mean I didn't have other talents. I was happy in your success and I had other interest. Anyway, what do you think?"

"Spirit Walker, all your spirit animals have come together to help you put them in the sequence." Moon Dancer had awakened. *"They seemed pleased with all the drawings, including the one you hold that Danene finished."*

"Well," she asked again.

"It's well done and that comes from a higher authority than me. Thank you, Sis," I say and then added. "We are going into Dad's study and I'm locking the door."

"Why?" Danene said in alarm.

"My spirit animals are going to help us with the vanquishing spell. We'll be safe. I don't want to be interrupted and have my spirits animals leave. Let the others know, will yah."

"Harley, will you come back into Dad's study. I think we can figure this out."

Rob and Josh were back, without Nakiya. They were both excellent trackers. I had wondered how far they would be able to go with it snowing like it was. Josh now stood at the window that had stayed intact when the patio doors had been broken. He stared out into the white abyss.

"Josh we are going to put this together," I say as I watched him.

"Sure, I'll be there in a minute," he said. Danene walked over and stood beside him. I heard her say something but did not catch all the words. Harley and I continued into Dad's study.

Placing everything on the large desk, I paused. Feeling all my spirit animals close; White Wolf, Great Bear, Snake, Raven, Night Eagle (owl), Mya (horse), Fox. I missed Shadow's spirit, which was between worlds right now. A few minutes later, the door opened and Josh stepped inside the room and locked the door. I laid out all the pictures Nakiya had drawn and the one Danene had drawn.

Most of them referred to releasing souls, the last the accession past the Milky Way.

"Open the book, Spirit Walker," White Wolf said. *Most chants of this kind have eight lines of incantations that must be spoken."*

"There will be one or two words on each page that will be used," Raven said settling his wings against his body. They will stand out when you read and we will catch them.

This was going to be a long night. I was thankful I had help in this direr time. Josh and Harley both had a pad and pencil to write down the words, for it sounded like they would not be in order. I started to read.

An hour later after listening to discussions from my spirit animals I asked Josh to read back to me the words he had written down.

"Smoke, earthly, calls, unharmed, powers, Icebis, cries, song, vanquish, name, rise," he said.

"I like vanquish," I say and turned to Harley.

"Free, mercy, retract, earth, place, victims, no, from, binds, spirits, leave," Harley replied smiling.

"Okay we have a good start." I continued to read while my spirit animals gave them the words to write down. Another hour passed and I closed the book as I had read it all at a slow pace.

"Okay, Harley you can go first this time," I say and put the book down in front of me. I looked over at Josh, his eyes were closed. "Josh, are you okay?"

"I was connecting with Nakiya."

"You can talk to her like I talk to Harley?"

"No, Kerry. However, I can feel her emotions. And right now they are neutral, so I know she hasn't been hurt," he said and sighed.

"She will be safe until the blood red moon reaches its peak in the night sky. Shawgun cannot do the ritual until that time," Raven said, and I passed that information to Josh. I was surprised to see Raven. He had helped me; however, he was not one of my spirit animals. "Josh is Raven one of your Spirit Animals," I asked.

"Yes. He is both mine and Nakiya's'," he replied

"Oh, that explains it why he is here," I nodded. "Go ahead with your list Harley. The faster we can put this together the quicker we can prepare to leave.

"Okay, he answered. "soul, powers, in, given, release, holds, this, of, give, now."

Josh continues reading, "now, you, home, this, soul, do, the; that's all they gave me this round. I guess now we have to unscramble them to come up with the spell.

117

"I believe the first words are, Earthly holds release you now," Moon Dancer sited. *"Write that down Kerry, and have the others cross those words from their list."*

I repeated the instruction Moon Dancer gave me. I was glad he had awakened. Our time together was coming to an end one way or the other shortly.

"I believe the next word of the new sentence is 'Icebis'," Fox said. *That's where we need to send him back to."*

"I think this next," Harley said, "'calls you home'."

Yes, that goes sound right, Icebis calls you home," Great Bear, agreed. *"The sooner we get him back on Icebis and hold him there the safer it will be for everyone concerned. Okay what's next?"*

"Powers smoke, no powers rise?

"Powers given now retract. Yes that's it, Powers given now retract," Snake hissed.

I crossed the words off the list and Josh spoke.

"Leave this place unharmed," he said with conviction.

"Okay what do we have so far? I ask.

"Earthly holds release you now, Icebis calls you home, Powers given now retract, Leave this place unharmed," Harley read.

"That sounds right," stated White Wolf *"Raven, you're thoughts?"*

"Yes, yes, go on."

We looked over the words that were not crossed off and then at the drawings looking for some kind of clue.

"I've heard him use these words and they seem related," Moon Dancer sited. *"Fire and smoke, fire and smoke cries from…"*

"This is a binding symbol?" Asked Fox

"It is at that. And that is what we want to do, bind his soul," Crow interjected.   Josh spoke up, and I could tell he was frustrated not being able to mind speak with the rest of us and only getting impression from Raven. "What are they saying?" Looking at Harley and me. I was taken back as I had never heard Josh raise his voice.

"Something about fire and smoke and binding the soul," I answered.

"You'll be talking to Shawgun when you recite this. Fire and smoke bind your soul. That's the next line," said Night Eagle.

"No mercy do the spirits give," added Snake.

"Cries of victims raise in song vanquish Shawgun from this earth," concluded Crow.

"Let me read it all back to you," I say.

> "Earthly holds release you now
> Icebis calls you home. Powers
> given now retract Leave this
> place unharmed. Fire and
> smoke bind your soul No
> mercy do the spirits give, Cries of
> victims rise in song Vanquish
> Shawgun from this earth."

"It is done," Josh said barely above a whisper.

"Yes and I hope it works or I'm going to be one dead dude."

"Kerry did you take a picture of the last drawing. You have to have them all as well," Harley said.

"I'll do that right now." I picked up my camera and placed the last drawing on a large white sheet of paper, and took the picture. "It won't take long to develop." Harley picked up the rest of the drawings and the book. After putting everything back in place, we left Dad's study.

"We need to get some sleep as we need to be well rested when we leave in the morning," Josh commented.

"I'll be in as soon as I get this picture finished and I've checked on Shadow, Josh. Goodnight."

"Kerry I'll go with you to see how Shadow is doing." Harley said.

"I won't be too long. Thanks Harley, I said walking into the darkroom."

"Shadow, are you awake? Can you hear me? There was only silence. Even Moon Dancer had gone back to sleep.

CHAPTER 9

When I walked out of my room, I had a welcoming committee in the kitchen. Everyone was there. So much for slipping away, but I knew better. My backpack was leaning against the wall, filled. I would still go through it to see what was inside. My brothers were sitting at the bar eating, Dad, Josh, Harley and Danene were at the table. My stomach growled at the aromas shifting around the kitchen.

"Here come sit down and have some breakfast," Jason said vacating his seat.

"How's Shadow?" I ask taking his place at the bar.

"He hasn't changed, Kerry. It is a waiting game. I wish I could give you better news," Jace said. "The goose egg on the back of his head has gone down slightly, his breathing is still shallow, and he hasn't opened his eyes."

Mom set a cup of coffee down in front of me. I could tell she had been crying. "Do you want ham, bacon or both with your eggs?" she asked.

"Both Mom, and some of your huckleberry jam on my toast please." I say waiting for the multitude of questions, I knew were coming. The mudroom door shut, Jace had gone back out. No one said anything. They just ate and I don't know what was worse the silence or being bombarded with question.

"Darn, Kerry, you expect us to just sit here while you hunt that thing down knowing he is setting a trap for you?" Steve cut through the silence like a hack saw.

"Steve, please," Mom begged. "Let him eat. You get him upset, he won't eat anything and he's going to need the energy," she said, a tear slipped away and ran down her cheek.

I took a sip of coffee ran my fingers across my forehead. I knew I had to eat and I had to stay calm. I turned slowly to look at Steve. "If there was another way I'd be the first to jump at it. However, there is not. Josh and Harley both know that they can only go so far with me. I have to finish this with Moon Dancer.

Dad stood up from the table and put his hat on. I had always tried to follow his example. He was a man of integrity in everything he did. Through him the strength of our family flowed.

"We'll do chores and let Kerry eat before anything else is said." He stated looking directly at me. He walked to the mudroom, Rob and Steve behind him. Mom set my breakfast on the counter. Josh and Harley took a seat on each side of me.

"I made this for the pictures, the paper with the spell and add a separate pouch for the magic rock," Harley said laying it down on the counter. "You will want to keep this on you in case you get separated from your backpack."

"Thanks Harley." It was made so the one side laid flat against my chest. I put it over my head and tucked it inside my shirt. "I'll be right back." I hurried to my room, took the photos, the spell and the magic rock, and placed them in the pouch. I looked again at the bear claw around my neck, the one thing that kept me safe from Shawgun himself, at least until the blood red moon.

"There's another storm coming in tonight," Josh said and then sipped on his coffee as I returned to my seat. "So the sooner we can leave the better off we will be. Danene says you know these mountains well."

"I know a couple of places depending how far we get, that we can get out of the storm. In fact, one place you can stay until I come back down from the summit with Nakiya," I say and started on my breakfast. *There was no other option.*

"Kerry," Mom said, "I've packed you food the same if you were going on a hunt, extra socks and long johns. I packed the same for you Josh and you Harley. I want you all back here in three days. If you need help, you can send one of your animal friends to us, can't you?"

"If we need help, yes I can do that," I say. I finished breakfast trying to map out our path in my mind. There were different ways up to the Cabinets depending on the snowfall. Trying to decide the quickest and the safest route to take with Josh and Harley was my main concern until I left them. Josh being a skilled tracker would not be in much danger in new terrain as Harley. They would have to stay together. Not saying that Harley could not find his way it was that his training was in others areas of their culture.

"Spirit Walker let me carry you up the mountain," Mya spoke.

"Thanks for the offer Mya. You have carried me on many adventures; however, this trip the snow is too deep even for you. If there is some way you can help, I will call for you," I stated.

Dressed for the winter hike I knew this would test the strength of my injured leg, I put the pain pills doc had given me in one of my zipper pocket of my coat, just in case. We were checking our backpacks when Dad and my two of my brothers returned from doing chores. Dad stopped to speak to mom in the kitchen and my brothers came into the family room.

"Jace doesn't want to leave Shadow. An added excuse not to say goodbye I think, however, he said he will see you when you get back," Rob stated.

Steve paced.

"Steve will you have knew doors on when I get back," I asked looking at the plywood blocking the light from coming into the room.

"I've already ordered them and don't change the subject," he replied coming to stand in front of me. "Do you have everything you need? I put in an extra box of shells in each of your backpacks."

"Thank you. It won't be bullets that will kill him Steve, as I said before."

"That may be true. However, you don't know what you'll come up against before you meet up with this demon."

"That's right," Dad said. "We've seen what he can do with animals he has turned. Even your mind speech had no effect on them. If you haven't mapped out a route remember you'll have a greater chance of an avalanche on the south side with this new snow."

"I have consider that Dad," I say. *I did know I was going to have to cross the face of the south side above the summit; however, I would keep that information to myself. My family had enough to worry about.* "I planned to go up past the meadows where we have tracked cougar."

"Good. There are a couple of places to get out of the weather if needed. That should take you a day n half to reach Snowshoe Peak area," he said and walked back to the mudroom. "I brought your snowshoes in and two more sets. They should be the right size for Josh and Harley.

"*Shadow can you hear me,*" I tried again, but there was still nothing. I put on my gear and Steve and Rob helped Josh and Harley get theirs adjusted correctly.

"I need help with one more thing Rob," Josh said and started down the hall. "If you would come with me."

It wasn't five minutes they were back. When Josh passed me, I saw he had the Sacred Arrows tied to his backpack with his bow. I recognized the cloth design I had seen near Wolf Talker on his deathbed. I had dreamed walked with Night Eagle and had watched Wolf Talker pass them to Running Wolf. These Sacred Arrows were passed down five generation that I knew of.

"Moon Dancer," I had felt him stir in my mind.

"Yes, Spirit Walker I saw them too. You will need them. My great great grandson is wise."

"I don't know how to shoot a bow, Moon Dancer," I said anxiously.

"When the time comes you will have the knowledge. Time is getting close I can feel it. I can also sense my great great granddaughter. Nakiya is cold and in a dark place. I sense her resolve to stay strong," Moon Dancer said.

"We will save her Moon Dancer and we will separate our souls. You have my promise," I opened my eyes when I felt embraced.

"You do what you have to do and hurry home," my mother said. "Beware of the fissure near Snowshoe, its depths go deep into the mountain," she whispered in my ear. I looked at her and nodded. I did not know how she knew about a fissure, as she had never hunted with us that high up. Nevertheless, her intuitions were never wrong.

I gave each of them a hug and I notice Danene gave Josh more than a hug, I smile, as I was not surprised. I had seen the sparks between'em the first time they met.

I left out the mudroom door and then put on my snowshoes as did Josh and Harley. The air was brisk. Snow clouds hung low over the mountain waiting to release their accumulation of the white fluffy stuff. We strolled just past the west carrel when Harley stopped us.

"I sense from this point on we should only use our native names, for we go to battle and if one of us do not make it back our spirit will rise and be greeted by our ancestors."

"I agree Otter. Let us pray to the Great One for courage and a straight aim against our enemy. That my great great grandfather will be liberated from this realm and he and Spirit Walker will find his last gift and vanquish Shawgun." Running Wolf raised his arms toward the sky and in his native tongue voiced our desire.

I felt my spirit animals near with the exception of Shadow. We trotted along at a slow steady pace over the flatland. Snow here was three feet deep looking at the markers on the pine trees dressed in white overcoats. We passed deer and elk that had come down from the highlands most clustered in the heavy thickets where the snow was thinner. I saw a stag stand proud on an outcrop he nodded.

"Spirit Walker, greetings. There is evil in the higher elevations. It spreads a poison over the land. Most animals have gone into hiding or moved on to other areas where the darkness has not crept in."

"I thank you mighty Stag for your warning. I have come to vanquish the evil that resides there. Have you seen two Blackfeet pass by here? A man and young women."

"There have been no other humans that have passed this way since the first snow."

"I thank you and may your life be long," I replied.

"Otter."

"Yes I heard the Stag."

"Running Wolf, Nakiya has not passed this way. Many animals have gone into hiding or moved their homes because of the evil on the mountain."

"Which way would he have taken her?"

"They could have followed the river," I say. "It would have taken more time because of the bends in the river."

We had traveled two hours and I was feeling the effects. I slowed and worked our way over to a large fallen tree where we could sit. I brushed off the snow. I didn't know what kind of shape Running Wolf or Otter were in, however, I had not hiked for a few months and with my injuries, I was feeling my energy dissipating.

"I was wondering if you were going to give us a break," Otter/Harley said and sat down on the fallen tree.

Running Wolf/Josh sat down and remained quiet. I suppose his thoughts were on Nakiya.

"In your packs there is a concoction Mom makes for us to use on the trail. It restores your energy and helps with your stamina. I have never asked her what she puts in it. I just know it works. The taste isn't too bad either. Here Running Wolf I'll get it for you," I said handing him my gun to hold. I pulled the bag out of his backpack, took one portion out, and gave it to him. I returned the rest and zipped it back up. I did the same for Otter and in return, he took mine from my pack.

"Thanks."

"Not bad," Otter said. "I can taste the alfalfa, bee pollen, and ginseng and wheat grass. I will have to get her recipe." I watched him put a small amount in his pocket and the rest back in his backpack.

"We have about two more hours of daylight, let's not waste it," Running Wolf stated and stood up. "Can we reach the shelter you talked about in that length of time?"

"Yes. If we push it," I say securing my rifle back over my shoulder and putting the rest of the small package of Mom's energy mix in my mouth. Picking up my poles and backtracking to the trail, we started north again. Snowfall was increasing limiting our visual ahead to thirty feet and that would dwindle when the sun settled over the mountain.

"Otter the hair is standing up on the back of my neck. I sense we are being watched."

"I agree. Keep up the pace, don't speak but stay alert, " Otter mind spoke bringing up the rear.

I could not see any movement but something was out there. Trying to conceive how to keep my poles and get my gun over my shoulder without tripping was a challenge. If we made it to the shelter, we were going to make up signs to alert each other of danger. Unless Running Wolf could feel the danger, I had no way to alert him. He could not mind speak.

Quickening the pace, I looked for the notched trees that were Dad's guide on cougar hunts when it snowed early in the season. They were carved with the letters JM six feet up from the base of the tree, and the trees were spaced thirty feet apart. That was about how far we could see. A heavy branch snapped in front of us blocking the trail.

"Go around Spirit Walker no time to move the branch from your path. Go to your left quicken your pace. The shelter you seek is not that far ahead of you."

I did not recognize the voice and I wasn't going to debate the matter. "Hurry we go around," I shouted over my shoulder as another branch came down to our right. I felt the front of Running Wolf's snowshoe clip the back of mine sending me forward. The snow-covered ground met my face first. I gasped for air, my heavy pack knocking the air out of my lungs. Otter and Running Wolf had a hand under my arms and for a moment, I struggled to get my feet under me. Snow plastered on my face burned and I had no time to remove it. Running was awkward with shoe shoes however, with the help of my poles I keep up the pace ahead of my companions.

I was thankful for the deep hard snow or our poles would have snagged winterkill on the trail. The butt of my rifle had loosened and through my clothing, I felt the hit on my hip with each right foot forward motion. It was coming dangerous close to falling off my shoulder.

"Spirit Walker I can see the cabin just ahead," shouted Otter.

The small cabin with its two bordered up windows and latched door looked like heaven. So close, as I heard another branch snap and fall. What was stocking us? We had felt the danger but nothing had exposed the form it took. I reached for the latch on the door lifting it up gave a push opening it wide as we all stumbled inside with the snow that had nestled against the closure. I see Otter quickly turn around shut the door pushing the snow back out so it would latch and lock.

"Did you see anything," I gasped. Still sitting on the floor, I removed my snowshoes and released my pack and rifle, as did the others.

"I could feel the anger and no, I couldn't see a shape of anything to know what we are dealing with," Running Wolf exhaled heavily.

'Same here…"

Otter stopped in mid-sentence as the shutters rattled and something scored across the roof. The roof and the shutters held tight. We stood up rifles in hand when snow dropped into the fireplace. Two mice ran behind the cupboard and a squirrel chattered at us.

"Sorry to invade little friends. We mean you no harm. I am Spirit Walker and these are my friends, Running Wolf and Otter, we come to vanquish the evil on the mountain.

"It's about time you come," he chattered. *"We are all in danger."*

"Let's get a fire going. There is fire starter and wood in the box," I say pushing open the lid.

"No, wait Spirit Walker. Whatever is out there could have blocked the chimney, in which case would drive us out of here with the smoke. Just sit tight for a while. If it could get in, I believe it would have all ready," explained Running Wolf.

The wind howled a threatening song, one that raised goose bumps. I put my hands to my ears. Fighting something you can see was one thing, you had a hint what to do to protect yourself. This was wearing on us mentally. Darkness covered us in its blanket bringing an eerie silence.

"Why don't the two of you try and get some sleep and I'll keep watch for a few hours," Running Wolf said. "I'll wake you Otter when I get tired. Spirit Walker you need to sleep. I notice you were favoring your leg as you ran."

"I brought ointment to put on your leg," said Otter.

"Thank you Otter. I will not deny I could use something on it. You would think that snow would be soft, but under the fluff, it's hard. I felt the impact when I fell."

"I see your cheeks may be frost bit. We did not have time to let you remove the snow. Besides you..."

Running Wolf stopped in mid-sentence hunching over he grabbed his upper arm, went down on one knee and sat back. "Nakiya!" He cried out.

CHAPTER 10

"Running Wolf what's happened?" I ask distressed. Otter and I both knelt in front of him.

He held his arm and rocked back and forth the anguish sliding down his face. Leaning over the arm that rested on his knee, he took in a deep breath. "He's dislocated her shoulder."

"He, who?" Otter and I both ask at the same time.

"Dark Antelope. I can only sense Dark Antelope and feel Nakiya's pain."

I stood up and hit the wall of the cabin.

"Spirit Walker injuring yourself again will not help Nakiya," Moon Dancer scolded.

"I know. I just feel so helpless when I hear she is being hurt."

"My great great granddaughter has many strengths. Keeping your focus is the way to help Nakiya. Shawgun will use your feelings for her against you. Only you can defeat him from those tactics by shutting off your emotions."

I stiffened my resolve and thought back to when White Wolf lead me to the plateau, and I sat across the fire from Moon Dancer. I smelt the sweat grass breathing it into my lungs and listened to him pray to the Great Spirit. I felt a calm I hungered for creep back inside me.

"I'm okay, Otter."

I heard Running Wolf say. I turned back around to face them. His face was more relaxed, and he was rubbing his arm lightly. I do not know if Nakiya could sense him not knowing the extent of their connection. What I had witnessed so far, I knew it was strong on his side.

"Take care of Spirit Walker's leg and I would check his knuckles, also. Then I suggest you both try to get some sleep. I can feel the wind coming from the fireplace. You can start a fire now if you want." He said so quiet it was like a whisper.

"Otter I'll build the fire first. I don't relish taking off my gear in this cold cabin."

"While you're doing that I'll get the ointment from my backpack," he said an amusing smile settled on his lips.

I stole a look at Running Wolf when he opened the shutter on the window partially.

"It's stopped snowing," he said. "It looks almost peaceful out there." He closed the shutter and walked across the room to the other window. Pushed up the latch and opened it. The light from the almost full moon swept across the floor of the cabin.

"Let's have a look at that leg," Otter said sitting on the floor legs crossed in front of the chair, I sat on.

The fire had taken the chill out of the room. I stretched my leg out. It hurt and there was bruising. Otter clucked his tongue and shook his head. He spread salve like ointment around the closed up hole of pink flesh and around the purplish color surrounding it and then put on a light wrap.

"You need to elevate this. Use your backpack that will be enough."

"Thanks Otter." I used my bedroll for a pillow putting my leg over my pack. I closed my eyes and recited the spell. *Earthly holds release you now Icebis calls you home. Powers given now retract leave this place unharmed.* What is the next part, think, think? I pulled the pouch from beneath my shirt that Otter had made me and took out the piece of paper the spell was written. *Fire and smoke now bind your soul no mercy do the spirits give, cries of victims rise in song, vanquish Shawgun from this earth.* I repeated it two more times, put the paper in the pouch and the pouch back inside my shirt feeling the bear claw next to it. The claw was my salvation and my destruction now.

The wolf howls woke us. Not knowing how long we had slept I looked over at Otter who was keeping watch. Running Wolf was asleep in front of the door. We both sat up at the same time. The fire was down to red coals. No one had bothered to add more logs.

"We need to leave before we get trapped in here," Otter stated. "They are still a distance away and the heavy snow will slow them down some."

It took only a few minutes before we were ready to leave. The clouds hung heavy waiting for a cue to release their contents. We needed to be to the pass before that happened. The pass was treacherous without the snow. Securing the cabin door we started up the undefined path the only guide were the notches in the trees and I knew they would be ending shortly. We could see Snowshoe Peak in the distance clouds hovering around the top. I quickly survived ahead knowing when it started to snow again the peak would not be visible and I needed to memorize landmarks.

The howls stayed a steady pace behind us, which made me feel uneasy. The colors before dawn were pushing back the blanket of night and I shivered. It was always coldest before the sun peeked over the mountaintops and with the cloud cover, only the strongest sunrays made it through, barely.

My stomach was growling we had not eaten before we left. As exhausted as we were last night, the thought never made it into our minds to eat or mine at least. The others hadn't said anything either.

"Spirit Walker can we take five and eat something," Otter asked. *"I've noticed that the wolves haven't shortened the distance between us the last hour."*

"I was thinking the same thing, Otter." I slowed down and stopped on the edge of a clearing. "Let's take five and eat something. I can't hear my thoughts above the growls in my stomach."

"Alright," said Running Wolf. "I've been trying to figure out why the wolves have kept the same distanced from us. What's up ahead?" he asked taking a wrapped package out of his backpack.

"There are the falls, a narrow passage that forks off to the trail that takes you to the south side summit of Snowshoe Peak." I say retrieving my own package. Otter was already devouring the contents of his.

"Is that the south summit your dad told you to stay away from cause of avalanche danger?" Running Wolf asked scanning the area.

"I have no choice but to go that way." I say looking in that direction. "Night Eagle said somewhere above the south summit is where Shawgun is hiding and where he will perform the blood sacrifice."

Running Wolf's jaw tensed. "I don't like it. Are we going across this meadow or are we skirting?"

"It would cost us time going around, however I don't like being out in the open," I say. We finished our food in silence just before we heard the wolf cries begin again. "Skirting we at least have the trees for protection. Let's go." With the snow level are pace was steady, however the wolf howls were getting closer.

We could hear the roar of the falls. Even in winter the river ran. On several occasions, we had good luck fishing at the bottom my brothers and me when we had clients with us. We started up the side using tree branches to assist us in the climb. It was slow going.

"Watch out," I yelled as I lost footing sliding back almost hitting Running Wolf in the face with my pole. "Sorry." I looked back the way we had come and that was when I saw the pack. "They're coming" I wondered how many animals Shawgun had killed to retain his power to posse the pack of wolves. We had protected them on our land. There was enough game that we seldom had trouble losing cattle to them.

Reaching the top of the falls the land flattened out and we picked up our pace. Unfortunately, it started to snow heavily again. I had a feeling Shawgun had something to do with that. The cold air I was sure would freeze my lungs. I could hear Running Wolf and Otter's labored breathing and wondered how much further we could go, that's when I saw it.

Had no idea how old it was or who planted the unusual tree or how it always survived the Montana's winters. We had built a shelter in it with a trap door.

"Up the tree," I ordered with no time to waste. I took out the extra box of shells and handed them to Otter before he climbed up. "This is where I leave you. You can hold them off while I go through the passage."

"Wait," Running Wolf yelled. "Take these you will need them to kill Shawgun."

I took the sacred arrows and his bow in their leather wrapped pouch and slung it over the opposite shoulder my gun was secured. Another moment to wrap my scarf around my nose and mouth before I forged into the pass. I could not see the wolves but I could hear them coming. Before the others could say a word, I left. Praying to the Great Spirit, that they would be able to hold the animals back and give me time to get to the summit. The distance I covered not far enough when I heard the first gunshot followed by a second and third.

"Don't look back Spirit Walker. Our mission is ahead, " Moon Dancer spoke.

"I'm glad you are a wake I was lonely by myself, " I said

He laughed. *"I'm afraid I haven't been that much company as I've tried to conserve my strength. I will be awake until we depart from here. "*

I wasn't sure if I liked the way he put that and I set it aside.

"We have come far you and I, " he said, *"You have learned many lessons that will enrich your life. "*

"Let's talk about that later and concentrate on what we are doing now. " I felt him smile when he agreed.

"What does this gift look like? It's not something I can swallow is it? I actually heard him laugh and considering the stakes this was not a humorist time.

"If gift is as I left it, Shawgun would have had no idea what it was. His only thought would be this, if it belonged to me and if he could hurt me by hiding it away, that was all that would matter to him. The contents resides in a smooth black leather pouch the size of the palm of your hand. Find the pouch and you will have found my last stolen gift."

We came to the bridge I had seen in my dream walk with Night Eagle. There were several old gnarled trees somewhat bare from the wind that reminded me of a gateway to where I wanted to go.

"Are you sure you want to cross that bridge?" I heard in my head. I looked around.

"That wasn't me," spoke Moon Dancer.

"Maybe it's my fear talking?" I say to him.

"No. It is not your fear. As right now, I sense very little in you. However, I would think twice about crossing that bridge. Did not Night Eagle warn you about the bridge?"

"Who are you, where are you?" I ask

"Look up."

I looked up mid-way and on a thick branch of the old tree lay a Lynx. Could this be my ninth spirit animal? His fur coat of browns, grays, and white strip under his jaw along his neck was thick. His ears had black tufts that I was told enhanced their hearing. His paws were webbed giving him a snowshoe effect in the snow.

"That I am," he said *"And as one of your spirit animals I'm advising you not to take this particular path, which may look safe to the eye is not, beside the fact this fall you would not survive. This is the intent of the demon skin walker."*

"I thank you for the warning. I have found that following the advice of my spirit animals is always the best path, I've learned." I say watching him come down the tree to my eye level.

"What shall I call you?" I ask studying him admiring his beautiful coat again.

"You may address me as Lynx," he said licking his front paw.

"Lynx."

He arched his back and stretched back his hindquarters. *"You and I will become good friends in the future. First, we must deal with the here and now and our time is short to accomplish what you and Moon Dancer have set out to do. Do not take this path but the one a quarter mile further up the trail. Follow me."*

"Moon Dancer, was Lynx one of your spirit animals also?" I ask watching the lynx trod gracefully up the path sinking slightly through the fresh power on to the hard-crusted snow.

"Yes, as he is linked to our last gift. He is the knower of secrets."

I did not want to know what that entailed. I had enough on my plate to deal with. I hurried to keep up with Lynx. My shoulders were aching from carrying my load and my leg was hurting. I had shut down my fear for now, focusing on my pain. I knew fear would show up later when I come face to face with Shawgun.

The snow was blinding. I could only see Lynx short tail and we were traveling to close to the edge to move faster. It was harder to breath, the air thinner the higher we climbed beside the frigid air seemed to go through my scarf with intent on freezing my lungs.

"Lynx, I'm told you were also Moon Dancer's spirit animal."

"Yes I was Spirit Walker. He would never say it, but I failed him, a mistake I will not make again. I thought he would foresee Shawgun go after his gifts, he did not."

"Don't blame yourself Lynx, I should have known he would try something on my accession," Moon Dancer stated. *"I do not blame you when the guilt is mine. Besides,*

something is destined to happen. We do not know all that the Great Spirit has mapped out for each of us. Spirit Walker would have hid his gift of mind speech with the animals from the world and he has much yet to accomplish for both our people."

"Why Moon Dancer, do you think my gift as you call it, is so important? I would not want anyone else to know outside my family and my three friends that I'm capable of speaking to animals"

"You have used your gift well with..." Moon Dancer stopped mid-sentence.

"We are here," Lynx said. "Follow behind me; do not move to the left or to the right. Walk in my tracks."

Looking at the cross over I would have passed it by, so unstable it looked. The crossing was about five feet across not much room for error. I kept my eyes on Lynx and walked in faith that he would get us to the other side.

I did not look back as I set my snowshoe on the south summit of Snowshoe Peak. Some winters the snow did not stick to the craggy rock face of the Cabinets. Nevertheless, somewhere up there was an opening that would lead me to Nakiya and Dark Antelope not to mention Shawgun. There would be more than one battle to fight this night.

An ache hit my heart as my thoughts turned to Shadow. I wonder how he was or if he had awakened. Was it just a spell on him? On the other hand, something more serious, I really did not want to go there. Shadow had been my companion since I was seven years old. We were teased that we were attached at the knee since that was his height. My eyes watered, a lump rose in my throat.

"Spirit Walker stay in the moment. There is nothing you can do for Shadow," Moon Dancer scolded.

"I know, Moon Dancer." Strange, I was use to Moon Dancer sleeping most of the time and my thoughts being my own.

"We have to react as one. It is our combined strength that Shawgun fears."

I looked ahead at the blinding glare of white crystals. It had stopped snowing, the clouds were scattered, the sun warming making the avalanche area more dangerous. My poles sank into the powder hitting the hard crust of earlier frozen snow.

Being on the opposite side from where we had started, I thought I was past the danger when I felt snow slide against my leg. Lunging for the tree branch as the flow swept my legs from under me. I was quick enough to grab hold with one hand but not quick enough not to lose my pole in my right hand. I held tight hoping the tree would not be swept away.

When the flow stopped, I looked for Lynx. I spotted him sitting on a snow-covered ledge watching me.

"Did you see that coming?" I ask easing down from the tree before working my way around to other side of it and then navigated my way to where he was squatted. Sticking my one pole in the snow after scanning the area above us for danger before I sat down beside him. Pulling the thin air into my lungs before letting it out slowly relaxed my tense muscles. I took off my backpack checking to see if the sacred arrows and Running Wolf's bow were still attached. My scabbard as well.

"Why would you stop on the edge of a possible slide?" he asked me back. My heart was still pounding. Putting my backpack back on and securing the straps around me, I said,

"Lynx I thought I was out of danger. I'll never be out of danger until I vanquish Shawgun, will I?"

"No Spirit Walker, nor will your family. Your brother Steve, though I do not know what special power he holds, has been single out by Shawgun. Shawgun must feel white power in him to attempt twice to take his life."

We heard gunshots again and then three quick shots. "A wolf has managed to get pass Running Wolf and Otter."

CHAPTER 11

"There are many places along here that give the impression of going deeper into the mountain. The one you look for will be marked with a half circle in black and one end will have a split snake head," Lynx said.

"Snake are you listening," I asked my spirit animal looking up toward the first possibility.

"Yes Spirit Walker," Snake replied

"I thought all snake medicine was good?"

"Snake Medicine is good when given freely and the opposite is true if taken. It stops the medicine from running its true course," Snake said. "You have no time for these questions now. Danger draws near."

Lynx scurried ahead of me and then I see him disappear. That was a fine how-do –you- do. I hurried as quickly as I could using one pole to push me forward to the cliffs going in the direction I'd last seen Lynx. The hair on the back of my neck stood up when I heard the wolf howl. Looking over my shoulder the wolf was closing the distance between us. I scanned around me finding a possible outcrop where I could brace myself to use my gun and not slide down the incline I'd just come up.

Crazy thoughts raced through my mind as I watched the wolf eat up the space between us."

"This is not the time to feel guilty shooting an animal," stated Moon Dancer

"His eyes aren't red," I said looking through my scope.

"Shawgun can hide the color from you. It's him or us," cried Moon Dancer

I took the shot. I knew I hit him but there was no body in the snow. The wolf simply disappeared. The gunshot echoed along the cabinets and I got a terrible feeling. I quickly leaned my back against the mountain under the small ledge as snow cascaded down from above starting another avalanche. I squeezed tighter into the crevice watching the rock I had shot from tumble down the mountain. The rock and the heavy snow claimed the bridge over the gorge and watching it collapse my chest tightened. Running wolf and Otter came scurrying out of the tree line. They had come after me, however now there was no way for them to get across.

Not wanting my voice to echo I only spoke to Otter.

"Otter go back to the tree house. You will be safe inside. There is no way for you to help me. Lynx says the other bridge is not safe to cross.

"Spirit Walker!"

I heard Moon Dancer call my name as the crevice I was wedge into widen and I fell backward into the mountain.   I tumbled repeatedly before I came to rest on

149

a flat rough surface. Pushing myself into a sitting position, before I moved further I looked around me. The crevice opening gave little light, a straight stream and that would be gone when the sun started its descent over the mountain.

"I don't think this is where we are meant to be," stated Moon Dancer

"Listen, something is moving up from the darkness." The scratches against rock told me whatever it was it had claws. "I really don't want to find out what it is and started to climb up toward the opening. The snowshoes were useless; I quickly took them off and hooked them on my backpack only to find my boots were not much better. The sound was getting closer and I was not sure what direction it came from. My pulse quickened, beads of sweat formed on my brow.

"Spirit Walker why don't you use your gift and fly us out of here," remarked Moon Dancer.

"That's right, I can shape shift." I took my pack off and set it in front of me. I determined the size of the opening and shifting into an Eagle, clutched the pack and lifted up toward the light. When it howled I did not look back to see what was coming to get us. In fact, the hot air coming from its mouth hurtled us through the opening just before the crevice closed, causing another small avalanche.

Flying above the mountain, I could see Josh standing on the other side alone.

"Otter where are you," I queried.

"Running Wolf sent me back for help when you fell into the mountain. Find a way to get him to the other side. You will need him."

My ego was not big enough to deny help if Otter said I would need it. True I was the one who would have to vanquish Shawgun, but who knew what else would stand in my way. I circled looking for a place to set down my pack and big enough area to set down Josh when I brought him back across.

Landing graceful beside Running Wolf, I shifted back the only way I could talk to him.

"I thought we had lost you when you fell into that fissure. I sent Otter back for help."

"I know he told me. He also told me I need to get you on the other side of this ravine as I will need your help."

"Spirit Walker I don't believe that an eagle can lift me over that ravine, chancy."

"What do you suggest Moon Dancer?"

"There is only one bird that can lift his weight. I heard stories in my youth and only once in my lifetime did I see one," Responded Moon Dancer.

"Can you give me a clear description, an image in my mind that I can hold long enough to get us both back on the other side?"

"Yes, I can do that. Perhaps you have learned about the Condor when you were in school, which would help."

"Whatever you two are talking about, make it quick. We don't have a lot of time here," Running Wolf stated.

Moon Dancer placed the image in my mind. I was startled. I had never seen a bird that large. I held on to the image and started the transformation. The condor (fill in the description) I lifted above the ground the height to grasp hold of Running Wolf with my talons. Flapping my wings harder to gain more altitude, we soared into the frosty air over the ravine. I set him down near my backpack without incident.

"I don't want to ever do that again," he said his teeth chattering. "What are we looking for?"

"We are looking for a half circle and at one end a snake head split in two. Should be drawn in black I was told."

"It would help if you could fly along that ridge. It would save time Spirit Walker. I have felt Nakiya. She is trying to hold the pain from me that she is feeling. We need to hurry."

I thought of the red tail hawk and the shifting was fast and smooth. I made three passes along the ridge of Snowshoe Peak before I spotted the symbol near an opening. I calculated the distance and noted landmarks that could guide us to Nakiya. I heard the gunshot and then I felt a twinge in my wing and started to lose altitude. I glided to the area where Running Wolf stood. My landing was awkward and after shifting, I saw blood. Just what I needed.

"I found it. I know how to get us to the entrance. However, it looks like he saw me, too."

"Slip your jacket off that arm and let me look at it," Running Wolf ordered.

Unlike him to use that tone of voice with me, I shrugged it off knowing he worried about Nakiya. I winced taking my arm out of the sleeve. Watching blood ran down my arm only to drip off my fingertips turning the snow crimson when it splattered. So much for flying for a while.

"You're lucky. It's only a flesh wound."

He stooped down gathered a hand full of snow and pressed it against my wound. I would have a scar to match the other arm. Maybe not, as this only took a small chuck of flesh.

"It's a good thing Dark Antelope isn't the best shot or you'd be dead," he said "Hold this here a minute while I get a bandage to wrap around your arm."

"We won't be able to use the snowshoes to reach the entrance. We can leave them here until we come back down," I say

"Is that too tight," he asked, "Bend your elbow, now straighten it. Good. The ice should have numbed it for a while and it will probably hurt when the numbness leaves. You have use of your arm and the Great One you should thank for that."

He was right; I didn't feel much pain now moving my arm around. If the pain was too much, I had in my pocket the pain pills doc had given me. I'm sure the freezing cold helped too. I shivered and quickly put my arm back in the sleeve of my coat.

"Thanks," I say. "And thanks to the Great One who we have our trust in on this quest"

He smiled slightly nodding his head.

"See that rock jutting out with three like prongs, that's our first marker we need to reach. Sorry we lost our surprise. No telling what they'll throw at us now?" I say while putting my pack back on and securing the front clasp. I had Running Wolf check the sacred arrows, bow and my rifle that they were still secure before I picked up my one pole. We started up the rocky stretch of mountain.

"I'm thinking it is a good thing I put a rope in my pack, Spirit Walker. I believe we are going to need it."

"I think you're right." Looking at the terrain ahead of us and the sun that had already pasted its zenith, I felt that we were carrying an hourglass and the sands were running out to fast. Hoping that when we entered the cave Dark Antelope had taken Nakiya, we would find her conscience. The thoughts of her on a sacrificial altar turned my blood cold. So much was at stake. Besides, each step we took drew us closer to a climax that would ultimately separate my soul from Moon Dancer's and the peace he would gain on Icebis.

Climbing toward the three-prong outcrop, we come to a halt where the rock was sleek. Hand and footholds were non-existent.

"Looks like it's time to use that rope," I say looking back a Running Wolf.

Taking his backpack off, he produced the rope from his pack. "Are you good with a rope?" he asked handing the climbing rope to me.

"We'll find out." Taking the rope I loosened the loop to the size I thought would go over the part of the rock structure that protruded from the base. Running Wolf ducked as I swung the rope above my head three or four times before I let it go catching the tip of the rock. Not sure, it would hold our weight, I snapped my wrist giving the rope a rippling effect hoping it would slide further down the rock, which it did.

"Was that luck or is that another hidden talent?" He took hold of the coiled rope and wrapped it around my waist.

"Champion four years running, but I had done very little rock climbing." I pulled on the rope it felt secure. How could I let Running Wolf climb up first not knowing what was up there. However, on the other hand his skill on this rock face exceeded mine.

"I'm going up first Spirit Walker," he said taking a knife out of his pack and sliding the blade into a hidden sleeve on the front of his jacket. "No argument. Anything could be up there and we do not have time to discuss it. He grabbed the rope started up hand over hand the twenty of so feet above us. Seeing him disappear over the ledge, I was relieved when there was no sound of a struggle.

"Okay. Tie the end of the rope to the backpacks. That will make it easier for you to climb and then we can pull them up once you're up here."

Securing the packs together, I looped the end of the rope back up to keep them straight. Having our guns hitting against the rock face was not an option I wanted.

"Alright I'm coming up." Starting up the rope, I winced as contracting the muscle aggravated my wound. Pain raced up my arm and I was determined to ignore it. Running Wolf pulled the rope up as I climbed. Less than an arm's length, I grabbed hold of the rocky edge and pulled myself over the top. It took Running Wolf no time at all to haul our backpacks up.

"How's the arm?" he asked looking up.

"I'm feeling it." Scanning the area, I looked for the next landmark mapped out in my mind when I was flying across this portion of Snowshoe Peak. "*Night Eagle I need help here. "* After Running Wolf curled the rope, attached it to his belt and checked our packs we put them back on.

"To your left a few feet and you will see what you seek."

"This way," I say walking the narrow incline. Snow was patchy on the rocks, ice base made the trail treacherous. My landmark a rope throw away had me worried. The cramped space would be a challenge to maneuver a loop.

"Spirit Walker on the other side of this formation you will find a hidden entrance, one not seen looking straight at the mountain, " Moon Dancer spoke with more strength in his voice than I had heard before.

Finding finger holds we inched our way around the cold granite. Sure enough, I could see a small entrance into the mountain.

"Yes, I remember this place. You will need your flashlight. For the first fifty feet it will be a narrow path."

"You've been here before Moon Dancer? " I ask taking my flashlight from my backpack.

"Twice in my youth, so very long ago. " He was silent for a few moments before he continued. *"There are several chambers connected throughout this web of tunnels."*

We followed the beam of light our boots scraping the path, our jackets the sidewalls.

"Can you hear that Running Wolf? It sounds like water running." Ducking my head under the lower ceiling of the path, we followed the decline.

"I can. There must be an underground river that flows through these mountains feeding the lake at the summit."

Our coats scrap along stonewalls. The promise our path would be narrow within the beam of light that guides us deeper into the mountain. Surprised our path looks worn the rock smooth beneath our feet.

"Running Wolf do your people use the mountain caves?"

"Not to my knowledge. I have never been here. I hope the path opens up soon this is a tight fit,"

"Moon Dancer says he has been here before."

"A friend of mine and I were following a mountain goat when we found the opening to this cave. We spent two days exploring. There are two heated pools besides an underground river that flows a short distance before disappearing into the mountain again. I took my father Raven Feather to our findings. We showed him the strange drawings on the walls none of which we were familiar. When we left the caverns, my father told me never to

return. He said some symbols were from the light and others from the dark side, " Moon Dancer concluded.

I repeated to Running Wolf what Moon Dancer had told me. We looked along the walls for signs or symbols hoping we did not miss any markings as we hurried along our rock path. Time was slipping by probably quicker than we thought guided by our flashlights. I was wondering how Shawgun was going to know when the blood red moon was at its high point. The time he had to make the sacrifice enabling him to become complete once more. Darkness lay ahead giving no promise of open spaces, and only silence with the exception of our footsteps.

Beads of sweat form on my brow as memories come to mind of the terrifying moments I have lived through because of this demon skin walker. My emotional roller coaster I had been riding for the last few months had not only put me in danger but others as well. I wondered how we had escaped in one piece and lived to talk about them. Well I guess not everyone had lived to talk about them thinking of the boy at the taxidermy school in Havre.

Glad that Josh was with me somewhere inside Snowshoe Peak was comforting. Loving Nakiya as I did was hard not to put her safety first. However, I had to leave her safety to Josh while I found the third gift and destroyed Shawgun. I searched for any contact I might still have with my spirit animals even my last one I had encountered, Lynx and felt nothing.

"You are strong," stated Moon Dancer moving to the front of my mind. *"You have the strength inside you to accomplish this task."*

I stopped at the etching in the rock running my fingers over it. *"You mean we have the strength to accomplish this task,"* I said. *"This one is the first one I'd seen, look familiar?"*

"Josh, do you recognize this?" I turned to the side not waiting for Moon Dancer to answer. Doing so, I brushed my injured arm across the uneven rock harder than I had anticipated. A moan escaped my throat. I thought I would feel Moon Dancer recede to the back of my mind but he did not.

Josh shined his light on my arm before looking at the etching. "Your arm it's bleeding again. There is blood seeping through your coat sleeve. As soon as we get into a larger area, I need to look at it again and change the bandage it looks like.

His light crossed over to where my hand rested on the wall. "No. This is no Blackfeet symbol. Listen. I can hear water flowing."

Turning my light back to our path I hurried following the sound. Our path curved and then curved back again bringing us into an open cavern. The water ran swift exposed the thirty or so feet before it disappeared into the rock again.

"Go back!" Nakiya screamed. "It's a trap.

We stopped dead in our tracks.

Chapter 12

Nakiya was on the other side of the river. A flash memory of a dream I had was before my eyes. She had been standing on that side of the river her arms tied behind her. She had not been hurt in my dream. Now, Dark Antelope held his arm across Nakiya's throat her left arm hang oddly to the side. A side of her face bruised. Wither she had fell or been hit I could not tell from where I stood.

"Nakiya," Josh yelled stepping closer to the edge his rifle already pulled from its scabbard and in his hand.

"Stay where you are Running Wolf. You cannot save her now. Shawgun has a higher purpose for Nakiya and the white man beside you who dared to partake of our holy ceremony will die tonight with her." Dark Antelope pulled Nakiya tighter against his body. Her face pinched as she cried out in pain.

I let my backpack down easy retrieving my rifle careful not to make any sudden moves.

"Behind you," cried Nakiya.

Turning around, another part of my dream came to life. I cocked my rifle and fired at monstrous grizzly standing not thirty feet away. As in my dream, the griz disappeared the bullets ricocheted. Nakiya screamed and Running Wolf and I hit the ground on our bellies.

"He taunts us," Moon Dancer said. *"You will only waste ammunition firing at him or get us killed. He cannot kill you himself until after the ceremony.*

Getting up on one knee Running Wolf turned his attention back across the river. "Dark Antelope you are on the council of our people, you are honorable, and the demon has put a spell on you. Let Nakiya go."

Dark Antelope shook his head as to clear it and took a step back. An instant later his body went ridged, red flashed in his eyes, his arm tightened around Nakiya forcing her to back into a tunnel with him a few feet.

"No! Think of your people. Do not dishonor them," Running Wolf cried standing up.

"Spirit Walker, leave Nakiya to Running Wolf," Moon Dancer urged. *"We must find my last gift and find the altar. That is where you will find Shawgun. Time is running out."*

Gathering my backpack, I put it on but kept my rifle in one hand the flashlight in the other.

Running Wolf had not taken his eyes off Dark Antelope and Dark Antelope did not lessened his grip on Nakiya. Time was ticking away and I had to act. Knowing if we rescued her now, Shawgun would not be able to sacrifice her, I....

"Spirit Walker, go. If I can't find a way across I'll follow you," Josh urged.

"Which tunnel do we take Moon Dancer?"

"Take the one on your right it goes deeper into the mountain."

I stepped into the tunnel my light shining ahead of me on the cold stone path taking us deeper into Snowshoe Peak. Adrenaline was high leaving in its wake the pain from my injured leg. My only thoughts were to find Shawgun, vanquish him before Dark Antelope reached him with Nakiya. The path I followed narrowed, the lose rocks I kicked over the edge I had not heard hit bottom.

"Are you sure this is the right path Moon Dancer?

Pushing my rifle strap over my shoulder gave me the freedom to feel along the wall with my left hand.

"Yes. The path will widen and it will split in two directions. You will stay to the right. Do you have something to leave for Running Wolf at the split if he didn't find a crossing?"

I thought of the red handkerchief I always carried in my back pocket. That would work.

"I have something. You must think he won't make it across the underground river if you want me to leave something."

"Only because we had tried and failed."

Not sure, of the time passing before our tunnel narrowed coming to a split in the trail. I took the red handkerchief out of my back pocket laying it in the tunnel we were taking. The path took an upward direction after a few hundred feet.

I stopped short and listened.

"Can you hear that Moon Dancer?"

"Shawgun has started the ritual. We must hurry."

My stomach knotted and the claw felt heavy on my chest. My quickening steps on the upward climb slowed and then halted. Turning off my flashlight heat escaping down the tunnel from Shawgun's ritual fire warmed my face and gave us a small amount of light.

"We need a plan Moon Dancer. If we charge in there, I won't have time to make the circle, spread the pictures in sequence and repeat the spell without him seeing us."

"That is not our first concern, Spirit Walker. We have to discover where my last gift is hidden. We find that and it will be simpler to do the rest."

Staying in the shadows my back rested against the stone. "What are we looking for? I didn't see any pedestals in the space ahead."

"The last gift won't be on a pedestal. It will be hanging in a leather pouch, perhaps hanging from Shawguns waist belt."

"Gee, Moon Dancer that sounds promising. You're sense of humor comes out at the most inopportune times."

"I said it could be. Shawgun not knowing the power inside the brown leather pouch won't be as protective of his prize."

"You don't think over these years he would have opened the mouth of the bag to take out the contents?"

"I'm sure he has. However, all he would see is a simple shiny brown stone. Even if he held it in his hand, which I am sure he has, he would not be able to unleash the power. He only keeps it because it was sacred to me."

The ancient Blackfoot Shaman in my head was generating energy. More energy than when he had let himself know to me. How much he had stored sleeping in the back of my mind I had no clue. However knowing Moon Dancer could only sustain that power for so long as I had experienced that transformation on Icebis when we found the blue orb. The blue orb, which gave me the power to shape shift.

Quietly sliding my pack from my back, I smiled, laid it on the path out of sight along with my rifle and flashlight. *"Moon Dancer, we can't walk in there and look around for the brown leather pouch as we are; but that doesn't stop us from shifting into something smaller Shawgun wouldn't notice."*

"Now you're using your mind. Small enough he wouldn't notice but large enough we can escape with it."

Picture of the small furry creature manifested in my mind. My bone and muscle transformed shrinking down to exactly the size I needed with claws that could climb the rock formation to view the sacrificial room. The animals black beady eyes scanned the room looking for the location of Shawgun and then preceded out of the tunnels protection. Shawgun danced around the fire pit his song dark and eerie.

"This is the only time I've seen Shawgun in his human form since that night I set the fire in the box canyon. His dress similar to what he wore that night," Moon Dancer stated. *"His fringed buckskin pants are painted in the same designs as before. The paint on his upper body has a few cryptic designs we found in Mr. Chavez's book. Two designs you have pictures of. Look at the sides of his stomach."*

Shawgun's face had one-side black one-side red and a wavy yellow streak down the center with black dots. The painted creature on his chest I did not recognize however, when his muscles moved it gave the impression the creature was moving.

Shadows danced across the walls from the fire and the only other light in the cavern filtered down from an opening in the top. I knew at once how Shawgun would know when the blood moon was in position for the sacrifice. I scampered up the rock until I was able to take in all the space below. We had gone unnoticed as he continued to dance.

"*Can you see your pouch?* I asked Moon Dancer looking over the area where Shawgun had his possessions laying.

"*No, not yet.*"

I could feel the frustration building in Moon Dancer and knew that escaping Shawgun would depend on his last gift or at least have a big part in us succeeding. My interest moved to the crude sacrificial block of stone. A spear was thrust into a crack in the rock.

"*There it is. Hanging on that spear,*" he said excitedly.

"*It might as well be hanging on Shawgun's body somewhere,*" I replied

"*Probably. Nevertheless, we know where it's at.*"

Silently stealing back to the tunnel where I had left my backpack, I saw Running Wolf. Hoping he had nerves of steel or any surprise we had would be over. Running over his boot and a few feet pass him, I stopped and shifted back hoping for the best.

"Seeing your back pack I wasn't surprised when the mole scurried down the rock and across my boot. Thinking you might have shape shifted." He said sliding his backpack off and setting it next to mine. "How's the arm. I didn't see any blood when you shifted back?"

"My arm is still attached,"

"I see you have acquired some of grandfather's wit."

Rubbing my arm, I said. "Now is not the time to discuss it. Where is Nakiya?"

"Wasn't able to get across. Dark Antelope pulled Nakiya down the passage and I am sure he is bringing her to the cavern you have found. I could hear Shawgun as I came up this passage." He stepped closer, peered around the corner and then stepped back. "He'll bring her here. Have you found Moon Dancer's gift."

Shaking my head and stepping back a few more feet, I whispered. "The altar. The pouch is hanging on the spear stuck in the rock. No way to retrieve it without being seen."

"We need a diversion, I..."

Running Wolf stopped in mid-sentence when Shawguns chanting stopped.

"Come out from your hiding, Moon Dancer. You think I can't feel your presence hiding in the dark?" Shawgun asked.

Running Wolf put his fingers to his mouth and motioned me to step back further into the dark.

"Come out. Are you still the weasel that stole my sacrifice and left my braves and me to burn so long ago?"

Running Wolf took off his jacket and slipped his knife into the back of his pants.

"No. Spirit Walker don't let him go!"

"Moon Dancer it's our diversion. Running Wolf knows what he's doing."

Running Wolf walked into the cavern head held high.

"Spirit Walker, unleash the sacred arrows and Running Wolf's bow from your backpack. Hurry!"

I scrambled to do as Moon Dancer beckoned and almost had them untied when I heard Nakiya scream. I laid them back down.

"Stop."

"Your right," I said motioning in agreement. Finishing untying the bow, I held them in my hand putting the backpack back down.

Looking around the edge of the tunnel, Running Wolf and Shawgun were on the far side of the room, Dark Antelope and Nakiya the far side of the sacrificial stone. Now was our chance to grasp the leather pouch and retrieve the stone.

I darted around the corner straight to the spear. Grasping hold of the bag, I yanked it free.

"Take the stone out of the bag," Moon Dancer *instructed. Hold it above your head and repeat these words. Light to dark, dark to light, make me invisible hid from sight. Repeat it twice.*

Again, I did as Moon Dancer bid.

Dark Antelope threw Nakiya against the wall as he ran toward us. His hand reached out passing through air the momentum slammed him into the wall behind us.

"Make your circle!" Shouted Running Wolf.

Taking the charcoal out of my pocket, I proceeded to draw a large circle. One large enough that the three of us could stand inside protected. The blood red moon was nearly directly over the opening. The sacred arrows glowed golden lying in the center of the circle

"Put the girl on the slab and tie her down," Commanded Shawgun to Dark Antelope. "I know you are near Moon Dancer I can feel your energy, still you are a coward." Shawgun and Running Wolf danced around each other. Both looking for a weakness.

"You dare not face me, but send your grandson. I'll let you watch as I kill your kin slow," he laughed and lunged at Running Wolf

My heart thundered watching Running Wolf jump back but not quick, enough as Shawgun's knife sliced through the material of his shirt not managing to find flesh however. I shuffled through the pictures until I found the first one to lie down.

"Spirit Walker tell my grandson Shawgun's knife is laced with poison," Moon Dancer spoke with urgency.

I looked up after placing the first card down. "Running Wolf his knife is laced with venom." I did not wait for a response before laying the second card down at two o'clock.

"No!" Shawgun cried out and stumbled back as if he had been hit in the chest. "No! Bind her," he shouted and struggled to straighten up.

Dark Antelope picked up Nakiya and awkwardly placed her on the stone slab. Pulling her injured arm up to tie to the iron hook, her screams shrill as the pain washed pale down her face.

My hands raced to place the third and the fourth picture in place. Shawgun went down on one knee.

"No, no it can't be. I will not let you win. My dark magic is stronger than yours," he cried pulling himself up. He swung around knocking Running Wolf to the floor before staggering toward the altar chanting words I did not understand.

"Dark Antelope you are a strong warrior. Take back your power," Nakiya, sobbed.

I laid the fifth and sixth pictures in place taking Shawgun to his knees. The spot on my chest under the claw was burning. The blood red moon centered over the opening. Shawgun's hand grasped the edge of the altar stone rising up.

The seventh and eight pictures were placed in the circle. Glancing up a flicker of recognition in Dark Antelope's eyes as Nakiya continued to plead with him. Shawgun's hold slipping to keep him under control.

We felt the power of the blood red moon flow down from the hole atop the mountain, Shawgun once again pulled himself erect, ambled along the stone were Nakiya was tied raising the knife above his head.

"Someone help me!"

I looked around for Running Wolf; he still lay where he had fallen when Shawgun backhanded him. There had to be black magic involved to knock him out. Dark Antelope slowly turned toward Shawgun.

"Take your knife and cut strands of her hair and give them to me," Shawgun ordered.

Dark Antelope slid his knife from its scabbard. Taking a fistful of hair, he put his knife to the long black strands.

"Please Dark Antelope. You love me, don't do this." Tears a steady stream flowed from the corner of her eyes.

Dark Antelope's hesitation enraged Shawgun. His face coloring made him more terrifying as his muscles twisted. "Cut it now," he yelled again at Dark Antelope.

Dark Antelope sliced his knife through her hair and handed it to Shawgun.

"Spirit Walker, pick up the bow and arrows and release your body to me."

Closing my eyes, it happened again. Moon Dancer made my outer appearance look like his. I knew when I opened up for him I would see the body of Moon dancer and I would be the one in the corner of his mind.

"Drop the knife Shawgun and step away from the altar stone."

"Now you show yourself you yellow dog. Your sister Spotted Fawn would have made great black magic for me but having your great great granddaughter will be greater magic. Your everlasting pain and her death will give me strength never felt before. Your gifts will disappear when I destroy your soul and there will be no rebirth for you ever," Shawgun grinned and the creature tattooed across his chest moved down from his chest to the altar stone.

"After I've killed Shawgun's physical body you will need to recite the spell to vanquish his soul. That has to be done."

"You call me a yellow dog when it is you who steals in the night killing and kidnapping young girls for your evil ways. You are lower than the dust my feet walk upon. This night I will be the Great One's right hand and strike you down."

I could hear the whispers of Nakiya still pleading to Dark Antelope. I saw him look at her and then at Shawgun, but his expression did not seem to change.

Taking the long ebony strands of Nakiya's hair, Shawgun rolled them into a ball and put them into the medicine bag that hung around his neck not once taking his eyes off Moon Dancer.

"She is mine and you have lost," he laughed and raised his knife."

"No," Dark Antelope shouted and reached for the Shawgun's wrist. "I will not allow you to touch my betrothed." They struggled but it was clear who was stronger even in his weakened state.

"You fool, you are not worthy of her," Shawgun shouted.

The creature bit into Dark Antelope's arm and he release his grip on Shawguns wrist. Still standing between the skin walker and Nakiya, he pulled his own knife.

However, Dark Antelope was not quick enough to stop Shawgun's knife from slicing into his own chest. Nakiya's screams filled the chamber.

Dark Antelope's hands went to his chest. His eyes wide with surprise that he had failed to keep Nakiya safe. He turned looked upon her face before he slid down the side of the altar stone and lay still.

The bowstring pulled back tight against Moon Dancer's shoulder, was released. His aim was true as the arrow penetrated Shawgun's heart and before we took another breathe a second arrow penetrated between his eyes. The creature screeched was shrill and horrifying loosening itself from Shawguns fallen body.

There was no sleeping and waking myself this time. I was thrown to the front of my skull and looking at my hands I was in my own body still standing inside the circle. The creature hissed on the outside of it.

"Now, would be a good time to recite," said Moon Dancer"

"Earthly holds release you now
Icebis calls you home, Powers

given now retract Leave this

place unharmed. Fire and

smoke bind your soul No

mercy do the spirits give,

Cries of victims rise in song

Vanquish Shawgun from this earth."

The shrieking wails of the creature turned to hissing, then there was only smoke before both the creature and Shawgun's body disappeared. Perhaps the creature was his soul.

Not waiting a minute, I was beside Nakiya untying her ankles and wrist taking special care with her right shoulder that was dislocated. The bruises on her face and wrist would fade away her shoulder would heal. However, the memories of the things that had happened to her would be another matter.

"You're going to be okay," I soothed "It's over." Kissing her forehead and each cheek before I held her close to me, knowing everything would work its self out.

"My brother?"

"Come sit by the fire and I'll check on Running Wolf," I say wiping the tears from her cheeks.

Helping her down from the altar stone and over to the fire was a task she was so weak. I wondered how I was going to get her off this mountain.

"Sit here Nakiya and warm up. I'll be right back."

Running Wolf moaned when I shook him lightly.

"What hit me?" He asked as I helped him sit up.

"A bit of skin-walker black magic I'm afraid. Does anything feel broken?

"No. I seem to be all together," he said patting his body. "Nakiya!"

"She's going to be fine, Running wolf."

"And grandfather?"

"I'm not sure. Wait a sec." *"Moon Dancer are you still with me?"*

"Yes, for a short while."

"He said he's still with me for a short while. Come to the fire and sit by Nakiya," I say.

"Wait. Will he talk to me, can I see him?" asked Running Wolf

"I'll ask. *Moon Dancer what shall I tell him?"*

"It will take a great amount of my energy but I will talk with him."

"I'm ready." I closed my eyes and receded to the back of my mind. My body transformed into not the young warrior, but the ancient Shaman that he was.

"Grandfather, I had so many questions I wanted to ask you, and now..."

"Grandson, know that I am proud of you and the path you walk. You have strong medicine for our people, as does your sister. You walk in the white man's world and you stay true to your heritage. Teach our ways to your children and their children."

"Grandfather, Spirit Walker has fulfilled the prophecy but you have given your gifts to him. How will this help our people?"

"His skin may be white, his heart is Blackfoot. Spirit Walker has talents that will keep our heritage alive and your friendship will stand the test of time. He will look to you for insight. My gifts of talking to the animals and dream walking were also given to Spirit Walker when he was born. The look of life we use in taxidermy, which, with Spirit Walker the Great One also gave shape-shifting. I will not question his wisdom. I..."

I could feel Moon Dancer's energy ebbing, his breathing shallower. I didn't panic. I knew he would switch before he endangered my life.

"Grandfather!"

"My journey has been a long one and I am tired," he said and put his hand on Running Wolf's shoulder. "You wonder about the last gift the Great One gave me that Spirit Walker has. The gift of invisibility. He will use it wisely and he will teach you to use it. Many changes are still to come for our people. Take the sacred arrows and keep them safe. Live with honor and be true to your heritage."

I opened my eyes and I was sitting across from Running Wolf back in my own skin. "Nakiya is by the fire. I don't know if you can put her shoulder back in place or not." I looked up at the opening above us. The red blood moon had passed over. "We will need to leave in the morning. What do you want done with Dark Antelope's body? He did try to stop Shawgun and was killed in the effort."

"His body will stay. We will place it on the altar stone where his spirit will guard this place from evil. He died an honorable warrior."

I nodded. I watched him move over to Nakiya. Closing my eyes, I spoke to Moon Dancer.

"You're leaving me aren't you?" There was silence for a few moments.

"Every good thing has to come to an end to make room for more," he sighed. "Thank you for helping me accomplishing my task."

"As if I had a choice," my lips curved up there was no stopping the smile.

"You always had a choice, just like you'll have a choice in the future. You have the heart of a Blackfoot; you will make the right one. Your friendship with Running Wolf and Otter will last a lifetime. Listen to the Great One and your Spirit Animals for guidance. This wisdom I give as I leave you."

"It will seem strange not having you in my head, I'll miss you,"

"My spirit will always be close to my family. Good by Spirit Walker."

I felt the last bit of energy disappear from the back of my mind but I could not help call out his name once more. Nothing, I was alone in my head. It felt strange being by myself.

CHAPTER 13

"How you doing," I asked Nakiya. I had heard her scream when Running Wolf put her shoulder back in place. She held her hands over the fire. It was dying down and I did not see a stockpile anywhere. All though the fire had lasted this long, surprised me.

"I'll survive. I've had enough adventure for a long time," she said and hugged herself. "I can't understand Dark Antelope turning the way he did. I knew how he felt about tradition however; a tree has to bend if it is to survive. His hatred for the white man and the loss of our way of life made him bitter."

Running Wolf stood over the body of Dark Antelope. "Spirit Walker, help me lift his body up unto the altar.

Positioning Dark Antelope on the altar, I reached over and closed his eyelids. Nakiya strengthened his clothing and Running Wolf placed his knife in his hands.

"I pray he'll rest in peace," I say. Leaning over to pick up the two sacred arrows I wiped them clean and gave them to Running Wolf. He would be there keeper now until he passed them on to his predecessor, hopefully his son.

Taking the knife out of my pack that Moon Dancer gave to me, I paused, ran my fingers over it before handing it to Running Wolf. "I think you should have this now."

He pushed my hand away. "No, Grandfather would want you to keep it. However, sometime I would like to learn how to use that stone. It could come in handy."

I felt the leather pouch in my pocket and smiled. "Sometime I will, if the need arises." I hoped the need would never arise.

Light filtered down, it was time to leave. Securing our backpacks, we turned on our flashlights and started down the tunnel Nakiya between us.

I squeezed through the entrance to the mountain. Perched on the rock where I had left him was my spirit animal the Lynx.

"I see you were successful in your mission," he said sitting up on his haunches.

"Yes we were and Moon Dancer has gone home to Icebis."

"Very good. I will leave you now. Help is on the way. If you need me again, call me."

He was gone in an instant. Nakiya followed by Running Wolf exited the mountain. It was lightly snowing and I was thankful there was not a breeze. Lynx had said help was coming I wondered when we would meet up with them. Not knowing how far Nakiya would be able to go in this cold as weak as she looked.

I stopped in front of her; her hood had fallen back away from her face. "Let me help you," I say. Pulling the hood back up around her beautiful face, I tied it.

"Thank you Spirit Walker."

"I think you can call me Kerry now. The mission completed. I'd rather be called Spirit Walker when we are among our people."

She looked at me oddly. "Our people?"

Grinning I slid my gloved hand down the small portion of her exposed cheek. "Yes our people. I have the heart of the Blackfoot. They are as much a part of me as my white family."

I thought I heard my name but was unable to see anyone.

"Kerry, did you hear your name. I'm sure I did."

Josh closing the space between us stopped. "I heard it also. Perhaps around those rocks we will be able to see. I hope that it's Harley with your brothers.

Josh had used our white names. Maybe he had heard me talking to Nakiya. We made it around the rocks and sure enough, it was Harley and my brothers. Getting over the ravine was still a challenge since the avalanche had taken out the bridge we had crossed the first time.

"We found a place for you to cross over if you can make it another quarter mile on that side?" Harley yelled.

"Night Eagle said it wasn't safe to cross," I yelled back.

"This one is a bit further down. We'll keep pace with you."

"Did you take care of business," shouted Jace shoeing behind Rob who was in the lead.

I gave him a thumb up. I remembered along here the avalanche danger. Turning back toward Josh "I think we should tie Nakiya to us. The area we have to cross isn't stable."

He nodded in agreement. Taking the ropes from our packs, we tied off. I was wishing I had not lost my other pole. Nakiya without poles to help her along was going to be difficult.

"Nakiya step in my footprints."

"Nakiya," Josh hesitated and then continued. "Nakiya would you let Kerry carry you across the ravine?"

She looked over her shoulder at him, "You're kidding right?"

I saw him shake his head side to side. Nakiya looked back to me her eyes wide and then back at her brother.

"No way. I'll make it across this snow cap." She turned back to me, "keep going I'm right behind you."

I continued on, using my pole to gauge the frozen snowfall we moved slowly forward. Harley and my brothers had moved further ahead of us on the flatter surface.

We were passing the bridge Night Eagle had warned me about when we heard the rifle shot and the sound echoed across the mountain. Someone was pouching. Feeling the shift under my feet, I looked around to find something to anchor us.

"Harley the snow is shifting. I have nothing to lock on to." I quickly removed my backpack. Removing the rope from around me and tying it to my backpack because I had the feeling I was going to need to shape shift.

I looked back at Josh he was trying to bury his poles in the snow for support. Lifting them both would be a challenge but I was determined to fly them to safety. There it came sliding toward us. I visualized the condor in my mind down to the last detail and felt the change start. Whether to try for the rope between them or for one of them...Josh would be able to hold Nakiya's weight better than she would his.

My wings flared out lifting me off the ground. Josh must have had the same thoughts when I see him nod and lift his arms up for me to clutch him in my talons. Nakiya screamed the snow sweeping her away until the rope when taut yanking her into the air as Josh was in my grip.

Flapping my wings to gain some height took everything I had. Getting high enough that I could catch the air currant to cross the gorge. That was my goal that I held in the condors mind.

Nakiya had stopped screaming. The thought that she had passed out occurred to me.

"Harley, I think Nakiya could be passed out. I'll try to land her gently my strength is diminishing."

The snow-covered ground was coming faster toward us. *I am strong, I am strong I can do this.* I felt a power surge through my wings the wind slowing our decent landing my special cargo safely.

"I have her Kerry and you were right she passed out. She is free. You can release Josh now. I opened my talons and released the rest of my cargo. Setting down twenty feet away, I shifted back into me. I was exhausted.

"Kerry you alright." Rob was the first one to reach me.

We looked up. The avalanche flowed down the mountain into the ravine. "We had no chance of surviving that," I say leaning back into my brother's arms.

Opening my eyes, I was surprised to feel my own bed. Shadow sat beside the bed but he seemed different.

"How you doing, boy?" I put my hand out to put my fingers in his coat and there was nothing there. *"Shadow"* I mind spoke

"I'm here Kerry and I will always be here but not on your plan of existence."

"No Shadow. Not you, not you." Wiping the tears from face was endless.

"You made it back safe. You and Moon Dancer accomplished what you set out to do. I'm proud of you."

"Shadow why now?"

"Kerry none of us can live forever and I was old. I have had the privilege of watching over you all these years. We went on many adventures together those memories will always be with you, as I will as your spirit animal."

"You were my best friend," I sobbed.

"Harley, Josh and Nakiya are in your life now and you have many more adventures ahead of you. You have a family that loves you."

"That may be true, Shadow. But it's not the same."

"I have left you something in the back of the milking barn. Everyone is still asleep. You can get dressed and follow me out."

It was dark outside and in my room. I turned on the bedside lamp and quickly dressed. I waited to put on my boots until I was in the mudroom with the door closed. My hat followed my boots and coat. I walked outside. The night was clear and a million stars sparkled. Following Shadow's spirit into the milk barn and to the back stall, I stopped short.

"He's the smartest of my off springs." Shadow said proudly. "Warrior, wakeup." Shadow walked closer to the small fur ball snuggled in the straw. "Warrior, wakeup there is someone I want you to meet."

"Yes papa." he mind spoke

"This is Spirit Walker also known as Kerry. He is also a brave warrior as you. One you will watch over."

I know my mouth hung open. He was beautiful as his father. I picked him up my fingers passed through his black and silver coat and I felt the calming effect Shadow had shared with me. I heard the barn door open and close. A minute later Mom stood in the starlight coming in the window.

"What are you doing out here?" she asked and then looked at the fur ball I was holding.

"Shadows?" She asked. "He brought him to you. He looks part wolf.'

I shook my head, choked up unable to talk.

"I'll leave you now. Take care of each other. I will always be close Spirit Walker."

"I'm sorry about Shadow, Kerry. Jace tried everything he could to save him. However, it looks like Shadow did not leave you alone.

"No he didn't. His name is Warrior"

She pulled her coat tighter around her. "A fitting name it looks like," she said walking back to the barn door. Why don't you bring Warrior into the house it is too cold out here. We're celebrating Christmas today with all the frills and bringing the presents out of storage."

Standing up with Warrior, we followed Mom to the house. "How's Nakiya?"

"Well enough for everything she has been through. I'm wondering what she will tell her parents when they get back from Hawaii."

"I don't envy Josh when he tells John's wife her brother is dead."

Mom opened the mudroom door and we stepped inside out of the cold. "I'm sure the spirits will guide him in what to say. For today, we will put all that behind us. I bet your starving. I have blueberry hotcake mix waiting to be used."

"You hungry Warrior. Your father liked blueberry pancakes once in a while." I set him down taking off my coat and boots. *"I have lots of stories to tell you about him. One for a long winter night with a warm fire and a cup of hot chocolate. When he found a hidden cave starting us on*

a journey to save Nakiya and Moon Dancer and vanquish a demon skin walker.

The end.

BLOOD RED MOON

JEANNE TAYLOR THOMAS

BLOOD RED MOON

BLOOD RED MOON

JEANNE TAYLOR THOMAS

BLOOD RED MOON

BLOOD RED MOON